HER FUTURE VAMPIRE LOVER

CASSIE ALEXANDER

CASKARA PRESS

Her Future Vampire Lover

Cassie Alexander

PROLOGUE

I heard the pearl before I saw it, rolling end over end against the jade tile until it tapped against my foot, shining white and as wide as a palm. I pretended to ignore it and kept reading my screen – it wouldn't do to let the servants bother me so easily, no matter that I'd been the one to teach them this method to get around strict protocol as a child.

I read to the bottom of my screen once, twice, and a third time – Yzin's latest story was about a dark world very different from my own, torn apart by factions fighting tyrannical rule. It had been utterly fascinating up until the distraction of the pearl but now I found my gaze slowing. Where I hadn't been thinking of pushing silk fabrics out of the way to touch and taste silkier skin before, now I could think of nothing but – and I knew Beza waited in the doorway.

I read another page, relishing the rising tension. As Queen, I could ask my slavegirl to do anything and she would. But the reverse was not allowed – which was why the pearl had taken the place of Beza's unspoken question.

Did the Queen want to use her magic on me?

As I waited I felt the answer to Beza's question blossoming inside, and a moment before she would take my inaction as dismissal, I rocked my foot on its heel to slide the pearl beneath my toes, rolling it gently back and forth across the floor. I heard her gasp and grinned, finally giving her my attention. She was biting her full lips now, the very image of hope restrained, and I swooped the pearl up in one hand and stood.

I could drop it here and take her by the bright glow of my screen. Or we could make a game of it, like we'd done when we were younger, now with very different stakes. I paced, my ocean-blue skirts trailing behind me, conscious of her watching.

My great chamber was the nexus of most of the palace's halls. The hallway to my servants' sleeping chamber was shortest, but rolling the pearl down it would be uninspired. Instead I walked across the room to the arch of the Hall of Ages, a hall so long I had only been all the way to the back of it twice before. I knew it had halls of its own branching off in either direction, each with rooms, shelves, and cases full of all the forgotten grandeur Aranda had ever had to display.

The fact that I, too, was on display inside my palace did not escape me. But I pushed that frustration from my mind, dropped to one knee, and sent the pearl careening.

It skipped over tiles of jade and amethyst and Beza ran after it in a swirl of orange silk, clapping her hands. She had until it came to a stop to run and hide. I closed my eyes and listened to the pearl wind down, bumping and rebounding off of walls and statues and when I couldn't hear it anymore I opened them. Beza was nowhere to be seen, but I would find her and then – I made a low sound and my secret place ached.

I picked up my skirts to travel silently, prowling like the jacars in their cages in the distant Hall of Living Things. Just like a jacar I knew what I wanted – and nothing was going to stop me.

Eons of Aranda's finest history went ignored as I strode past antechambers and branches. During my three hundred years of living in the palace my servants and I had exhausted all of the easiest hiding spots, and besides, it would be insulting for Beza to hide nearby when I had rolled the pearl so far intentionally.

An eight-legged zoomer crawled up the hall faster than I could walk, off to scrape up some piece of dust that only it could see. It or one just like it would eventually return the pearl to the pile of gemstones in my room where it'd come from, gifts from my councilors after one of their interminable meetings. If the council knew what I was using the pearl for now – I felt myself flush. As Queen, I could do what I liked inside the palace, but I knew from the screens Yzin gave me that Queens ought not to know their servants quite so well.

And as if to remind me of that fact, I walked past the chamber holding the statue of my King. I paused in his doorway, looking in. He was just as stern as the moment he'd been unveiled, a Zaibann warrior of my very own, trapped in stone until our wedding ceremony released him. He'd been chosen specially for me by the council's celestitians, and I knew nothing about him except what I could see – his imperious gaze, his strong chin, his broad chest, and then, like a fertility deity of old, his erect stone cock, jutting out from between the folds of his statue's armor.

Seeing him turned my thoughts to the night that I'd discovered that I was magical – and it made my need for Beza grow.

The halls held more statues, delicate arrangements of exotic flowers, elaborate rugs beaded with gemstones both hung on walls and walked on, fabulous paintings of successful generals and queens from before written history. Glasswork cages held mechanical and living lilans, singing the same songs in harmony. Hall after hall of beauty and I ignored the lot of it – what Beza offered was more precious than any of the art or jewels I passed.

Places inside me ached to be touched and filled, my skin longed for the feel of her skin brushing against it – my patience waned as my need roared. I didn't want to play fair any longer, it was time to use my powers. I closed my eyes, steadied myself, and felt out.

Feeling was the only word for it, though I didn't use my hands. I sent a part of myself that I couldn't describe out to search for Beza, and soon I knew without being able to say how that I should turn right.

I took a few steps down the right-hand hall, and stood in front of the Chamber of Vased History. My magic tugged at me again, like low hands pulling at my hips, and I opened the door to step inside.

It was a massive room, full of styles of pottery from all of Aranda's ages. I couldn't recall anyone ever hiding in it before which was a shame; it was a perfect place, full of bulky jars and squat pedestals to hide behind.

The vase at the end of the first row was almost big enough to hold Beza – it was as tall as I was, and the dark red color of blood. I could see the streaks its creator's fingertips had left on its surface as I neared, my magic pulsing inside me with every step, pulling me toward what I desired.

I still wasn't used to having power – I worried that it would leave me, or that I was imagining things. So I crept closer slowly, hoping that my magic was true. I wanted it to be – I ached for it to be – so when I saw a tickle of orange fabric peeking out from behind the vase's base it was hard not to gasp with relief.

I pulled up my skirts and walked along lightly, controlling my breath. My servants had minds of their own and had played tricks on me before, disrobing and leaving gowns behind like shed skins to race away naked, laughing at momentarily fooling their Queen.

But more often than not when we played this game now whomever was found chose not to run very far – because being caught was what made the entire game worth playing.

I whirled around the vase, surprising her. She startled and then laughed, clapping her hands to her chest, still breathing hard from her run.

"I've found you," I said, trying to sound imperious.

"You have, my Queen." Her lips parted in a wide smile.

There could be 'punishments' for running – but more often there were rewards. My breath was loud in my ears now, from the thrill of her discovery, and knowing full well what I could do with her next.

"Kneel," I commanded, and Beza did so in an instant, head bowed, hair the color of the vase behind her slipping forward of her shoulder to hang in a smooth wave.

I thought then of pulling up my skirts and putting them over her, presenting her with my darkest place, feeling her hands push my thighs open until she could lick the sweetness out of me – but, no – sometimes it was better to give than to receive. I put one slippered foot on her shoulder, waited the length of a breath, and then lightly pushed her back onto her rear.

Beza went with the motion and fell back with a soft surprised sound, her back thumping lightly against the vase. She looked up, eyes shining, and I sank to meet her, kneeling, my azure skirts swirling with her orange ones. The colors merged like a sunset and it was easy to find her orange skirt's hem. Pushing it up revealed skin every bit as luminous as the pearl had been.

"My Queen," she whispered in hope. Protocol still said that she could ask for nothing, and there was no pearl to be her messenger this time. But I knew what she longed for – and I leaned forward to kiss her.

There was such a difference between kissing Beza and Joshan. Joshan's kisses were strong, his lips heavier, while Beza's were more softly yielding. I pushed my tongue into lovely Beza's mouth and tasted her as she made gentle sounds, and felt her breath quicken as my hands slid higher.

I had thought I'd known what it meant to rule before I'd kissed Beza but truth be told, trapped inside the palace, taking control of Beza's desire was the first time I'd ever felt like a Queen.

I pulled back as I pushed the final few inches of her skirt up, so that my slavegirl was completely exposed to me, watching her face all the while.

"My Queen," she whispered again, breathing hard.

"My darling Beza." There was a secret, dark place that she and I shared, and we hadn't known until recently what could be done with it – but now that we knew, there was no turning back. "Would you hold back my hair?" I asked, and she nodded. Knowing what would come next, she spread her legs wide.

I sank my head down reverently and pressed my lips to the petals between her thighs, kissing them until they opened and her honey ran out, and she stroked my hair back with a moan.

Her voice rose under my attention, and by now I knew the fastest way to release her, but I didn't want this to be over so quickly. Instead I buried myself in Beza's lap, in the taste of my girl, the scent of my girl, the heat radiating off of my girl's thighs. And for her part, my servant breathed heavy and moaned, rocking her head back, joyfully losing herself to her Queen's desires. I purred in pleasure at pleasing her – looking up at her with her head tossed back, feeling her fingers tighten against my scalp as they pulled my hair. Yes – that – something about it – my magic swelled in me and suddenly I needed more, much more. I pulled up, Beza's honey slick against my lips.

"My Queen?" Beza asked, lost eyes trying to focus on me.

"Just a moment," I said, and snapped twice for Joshan.

Some days I made him watch, pretending to be oblivious to the erection which his uniform did not disguise, other times I would rock back and make him take over, watching him and Beza as I satisfied myself. And still on other days – when he came into the room, I reached back and flipped my voluminous skirts up, revealing my own dark place to him. "I need you to service me."

"My Queen," he acknowledged, and knelt down.

He would do anything I asked – which was good, because his cock fit my dark place perfectly, hitting spots inside of me my fingers never could. I crouched in front of him, panting for a few eager moments as he readied himself and then – I moaned low as his cock slid inside. I held myself there until he began to stroke me, relishing the sensation of him pushing in and pulling out, before I bowed back down to Beza's lap.

What we were then, I couldn't say. I licked and sucked at Beza's petals, rolling her folds across my tongue, pushing her open, and then sucking up as if I could pull all the sweetness from her, me rocked all the while by each stroke of Joshan's cock. I was trapped between them, taking what I wanted from my willing Beza at the same time Joshan answered all my needs.

"My Queen, my Queen –" Beza writhed and moaned, her voice as melodious as the birds chiming the hour outside as her moment neared. "My Queen, Queen – Queen –" she shouted and screamed, hips roiling under my mouth, as I greedily sucked at her, before she collapsed on the ground beside the vase, in a tangle of orange.

Now it was left to Joshan. I braced harder to take more of him in, and the servant rocking behind me moaned. It was his sole job to see me satisfied, and he had never let me down. Each thrust made him fill me and still wish for more, and it was my turn to sound like Beza had, shouting low with each thudding stroke.

And then Beza's hands were there, reaching out to hold my breasts, stroking my nipples through my dress's thin gauze. I looked up at my serving girl's face, and kissed her for knowing what I needed more than I did myself, as each deep push made my breasts sway.

"More, Joshan," I ordered, and my servant redoubled his efforts until I was falling forward, now held up by Beza as my girl reached back to rub the spot between my legs. These new feelings, being trapped and held and pinned and stroked, my breath hot on Beza's neck as I clung to the girl who rubbed me right where Joshan's cock was entering me so hard –

I cried out helplessly, suffused with power, roiling between the two. Beza held onto me but didn't stop, and neither did Joshan, until I sagged to the ground between them.

Beza rocked back roughly as Joshan rocked forward, and the vase – already jostled from Beza's time – tilted precipitously, until it fell off of its stand away from us, shattering loudly into a million precious bits.

Both the servants startled at this and looked to me. I gasped in surprise, and then laughed. At that, both of them laughed too, all three of us in a tangle of wild fabrics and shards of irreplaceable ancient pottery.

This was life in the court of the Feather Palace, in the time of the Unfurling Lotus, year twenty-three thousand four-hundred and one.

1

Eventually I stood, pushing layers of gauzy blue back down. Beza was disheveled, orange skirts still high, and Joshan, ever patient, was hard and ready just in case his services were still required.

"Beza, finish him, will you?"

My serving girl nodded, and set to working at Joshan's cock with her mouth.

I breathed in and out deeply, watching her enthusiastic work. Joshan's eyes were on me should I need him but I shook my head and watched the man dissolve in bliss. I knew just how good her tongue could feel, and didn't want to interrupt his pleasure.

They would have to be quick, though. A squad of zoomers would be here shortly to fix the mess we'd made. I knelt down to pick up a pottery shard. I couldn't say how old the vase was, there was too much history to choose from, I only knew I'd never noticed it before. I turned the blood red piece over in my palm. Funny how the vase was more interesting after it'd been broken, then when it'd been one among the many of its kind.

I heard Joshan's grunting mount and watched him. Beza was crouched over his hips, mouth open, jaw dropped, taking his cock as he thrust it. His hands clutched out, found her hair, then he shouted, bucking in spasms, until he was through and gently pushed Beza back.

"Satisfied?" I asked, smiling down.

"Of course, my Queen," he answered.

Watching them made me think of asking for more, no matter that I had been so recently sated. We had spent days like this before, taking turns, two making the other one scream.

But I could hear zoomers coming down the hall – and overhead announcement chimes rang, the tones picked up and echoed by real and mechanical lilans throughout the palace. A council visit – and we only had the time it took for the council to mount the thousand-step stair to prepare.

I looked around at our disarray. If I had had more warning, I would bathe and be anointed with oils, put on fresh clothing, and choose one of the necklaces of my office to wear. Now, though – I knelt, and Beza began rebraiding my tangled hair. It would be easier with a brush, but it would take too long to fetch one now. Joshan tucked his cock away and set to straightening out my robes just as the first of the zoomers entered, and anything we might have said to one another was impossible to hear over the sound of their sharp teeth grinding pottery.

Yzin was the only councilmember I liked. They were all old and stodgy, and each had their own way of taking up all the air in the room – I'd had to listen to each of them during the countless cere-monies we attended in assorted chambers, me sitting perfectly still as my image was projected to a thousand-thousand screens outside. Yzin was the only one who seemed to care about me – he'd taught me history, up until he said there wasn't anymore, that we were making it ourselves – and he'd taught me how to read, then brought me screens to read for pleasure. Out of all the gifts the councilmen brought me, his were the only ones I enjoyed.

One of the nearby zoomers ground to a stop, finishing the piece it held, reaching a paw out for more. Lifting a bigger shard revealed an unfamiliar object – I lunged for it and snatched it out of the zoomer's path.

"What is it, my Queen?" Beza asked, looking over my shoulder at the thing. It folded open in all sorts of places and had strange and rough designs.

"I don't know." I hid it inside my dress, along with the shard of pottery I held. Maybe I could ask Yzin about them.

"The council waits, my Queen," Joshan said, offering me his hand. I took it, stepped around the zoomers that now outnumbered the pottery shards, and made my way outside.

WHEN I REACHED my council chamber, I could hear my counselors talking outside the chamber door. They weren't speaking my tongue, but I understood it all the same. I assumed they had their own language, just as the lilans spoke to one another in their cages, like calling like. I had wondered how come I could understand them, though, and not the lilans. As a child, I'd have found understanding lilani far more interesting.

"Must we?" I heard Yzin ask.

"You know we must," Railan answered. "You should want this more than anyone." And then one of them rapped on the door three times, the doors opened, and the entering ceremony began.

It was always the same. Servants paced in, singing that I embodied all that was magic and holy in the world, how my beauty shone through the ages, and how being in my presence was like being in the light of the sun.

As I had never seen the sun, I had to take their word for it.

I waited my turn, then walked to my throne on a dais in the center of the room. The council members fanned out around us, each flanked by two servants, walking at a stately pace. Overhead, the glass stalactites glowed in warm shades, and the screens lining the walls showed pictures from Aranda's countryside, gentle scenes of mountains, oceans, and distant towns, the countryside and cityscapes I ruled.

I had begged to visit them as a child, and been told I was too precious to leave the palace, even for a moment. In time I'd come to accept that the pictures of Aranda were all I'd ever see.

Railan finished his walk last to come and kneel at my feet, his red robes dragging behind him and long sleeves spooling out. I noticed, not for the first time, that his robes were embroidered with gold lilans in flight, and wished there were a way for me to see such a thing. The ones in my cages all had clipped wings.

I waited a long moment, looking around at my councilmen, their golds and purples, sashes and headwraps set with jewels, kneeling one by one. Last of these was my Yzin, who was having problems performing the task.

"Please, stand," I implored him, at seeing him struggle to bend down.

He looked at me with a face tracked with so many lines it could have been on the wall of the Map Room, and pressed a hand to his chest. "My Queen, I am humbled by your consideration."

"As I am by your presence," I said in return, pressing a hand to my own.

Railan cleared his throat, looking over at his fellow councilmember dourly, before looking up at me. "Queen Ilylle," he announced.

"High Councilman," I acknowledged him.

"You are well, yes?" he asked, eyebrows high. He sounded sincere, but I thought I detected the hint of a smirk in his tone.

Could they tell what I'd done with Beza and Joshan? Did they know? I bit the inside of my lip, and then set my shoulders. It didn't matter if they did. I was royal, and inside the palace I could do as I liked.

"I am very well, as always. How could I be otherwise, with you at my feet?"

Railan blinked at this response, and I stifled a smile as he pressed on. "We are here to inform that the celestitians have decreed the date of your King's arrival – you are to be married eleven days from now, on Tide's Day."

It was my turn to blink. "I...am?"

Railan nodded gravely. "We wanted to give you time to ready yourself. You already know the traditions you have to uphold."

I'd read about the ceremony a thousand times – the day of ceremonial bathing, incense, prayers, and then my wedding to the statue in the chamber. A choir would sing, I would join their song, and he would come back to life. Together, we would go on to rule Aranda side-by-side.

It was only at the back of one of Yzin's most recently gifted screens that I'd found a different tale, one that insinuated that what woke their Zaibanns wasn't a Queen's singing, but her taking his hard stone cock into her soft dark place. The thought both horrified and thrilled me.

"Does this please you, my Queen?" Railan asked, with a look of concern.

I roused from my thoughts and quickly smiled down. "Of course it does. It is how it has always been, is it not?"

"Indeed." Railan nodded again and stood. "We have a new screen for you to read, Queen of Dreams."

"You do?" I forgot to hide my excitement. It had been a long time since their last request.

"We do," Yzin said, kindly. He handed it over and it lit up at my touch. My eyes skimmed the words – these screens were the only communications I had with my people. The people of Mazaria – a southernly region – were rioting, and needed to be calmed.

"But – why?"

Railan stepped nearer, and pressed both his hands to his chest. "A terrible drought has caused crops to fail. Certain officials tried to hide the extent of the disaster, and our response has been correspondingly slow."

"But now? We're doing all we can?"

"Of course, my Queen. Supplies are being sent. We just need them to be patient."

Yzin smiled at me. "Not even the Queen of Dreams can control the weather."

I swallowed and nodded, standing up so that my voice would ring clear, as the lights on the glass stalactites brightened. I held up the screen and read what it said. "To the people in Mazaria, please calm yourselves. Your officials are doing what they can to remedy your situation. Be prepared to present identification to officials when asked, and stay indoors after dark." The official message ended there, but I continued. "I promise you that supplies are being sent. Be patient, and know that I think of you."

I sat down as the lights faded – and could see that Railan's jaw was clenched. "Dearest Queen, you're supposed to say what it says on the screen, no more, no less." His voice was high, speaking to me as he had when I was a child.

"No harm was done," Yzin said. The other councilmembers looked to one another and muttered expressions of shock and dismay.

They were...upset with me? But – they were in my palace. And I was Queen. I handed Railan his screen back primly. "Was there anything else, High Councilman?"

"No, of course not, Great Queen." He took the screen and folded it into a pocket. "We shall see you again at Tide's Day."

"I'm already looking forward to it," I said with a gracious nod.

He left the first gift in the basket near my feet. It was a scepter, a simple gold tube with an emerald the size of an eye at the end. The others dropped off their gifts one by one, wishing me health and prosperity as I wished it back on them. A pile grew, a wreath of what were no doubt exotic lilies, two silver tskiss trapped in an appropriately silver cage, a rug of gold embroidered with silver and hung with nightdark beads, and more gemstones, each carved more elaborately than the last. I pretended to be pleased to accept them, all the while knowing that once the zoomers had cleaned and organized the chamber I might never see them again, that they would be lost in the other piles of rugs and gemstones and flowers the Feather Palace held.

Finally, only Yzin was left. He, as always, held out a screen.

"What is it today?" I asked, while reaching into my pocket for the pottery. My fingers brushed the other object that I'd stolen from the zoomers. I would have brought it out, but other council members still stood nearby and I only wanted to show it to Yzin.

He pressed his wrinkled hand to the back of the screen. "A new story, written just for you."

I could not tell him what his gifts meant to me while the others were near, but I hoped he could read it in my eyes. His stories occupied my mind in a way that none of the baubles the other Council members gave me could.

"Thank you," I said, with feeling.

"You're very welcome, my beautiful dear," he said.

I brought the pottery shard out before he could step back. "We broke this. Was it important?"

He took the piece and eyed it carefully. "I don't know, child. I can research it for you and come back, however."

"Please do."

He nodded and smiled and tucked it into one of the pockets of his own robe, and then followed the rest of the council members on their way out. I sat still on my throne until the doors closed behind him and I was left inside the Feather Palace alone with just my servants again.

I'D TRIED to follow the Council out more than once as a child. I'd been prone to impertinent questions then, always asking *why?*, and *how come?* It wasn't until Yzin had started teaching me that I began to understand the way that things were done, and learned that even a Queen could not change certain things, no matter how much she might long to.

I stirred the gifts they'd given me with a toe. Zoomers would be here soon – I stood and took the scepter after a second thought.

Tide's Day – just eleven days. Would things change then? Yzin's books never said what happened after the ceremony, and he'd never satisfactorily answered when I'd asked him. Everything he'd given me to read recently had been fiction, not history. He always said it was because my King and I would set my own course and rule as we desired.

What if we desired to leave the palace? Would it be allowed then? Surely I would be safe outside the palace's doors with my King at my side. He was a warrior, after all.

I walked down the halls wondering on this, and when I would next get a chance to privately ask Yzin, slowly heading back to my great chamber, past my King's open door. I paused again to look in at him, taking in his form, remembering that first night with Joshan. I felt a low pull, the beginnings of my magic stirring deep inside of me, and stepped inside.

"Do you know that in eleven days you'll be my King?" I asked him. I'd taken to addressing him as a person as a way to alleviate my fears. Who was he? What kind of man would he be, once released from stone?

I'd been wondering those questions for months now, ever since the celestitians had chosen him. There were five thousand stone warriors trapped in their chamber far below – how did they know he was mine?

Zoomers the size of urshaks had brought him up from the Zaibann Chamber's depths and carefully placed him in this room – a room until then whose emptiness I had never questioned, in retrospect. All of the council members were present, along with their families and selected slaves, and there'd been a great feast at the long table set up in the room in front of him. I sat beside the stone statue and everyone cheered and chatted and was kind to me – even Railan. I was unused to so many people talking to me all at once, but it was delightful. Everyone was so happy for me, how could I not be happy for myself?

It was only later during the terrible silence after their departure that I could hear myself think enough to have questions – questions that had never been answered since.

At the time, I thought I had to trust in my council. But soon after that I learned about my magic on the floor in this room – and now I was learning to trust in it, too.

Which was why when it brought me into the Zaibann's chamber I didn't question it. I stood there, looking up at him as I often had. He would be someone to talk to, to dance with, to sleep by at night. I wondered about so much of him – how he'd act, who he'd be – what it would feel like to be near him. I wondered too if, in his own slow-stone way, he was equally curious about me.

"Are you ready to live again?" I asked. Of course he didn't answer.

He'd seen us in this room before, playing, practicing – as much as anyone who was stone could – but this time I wanted him to see just me.

I set the screen down but held onto the scepter. This was definitely not why Railan had gifted it but my magic wouldn't be denied. Not when it was thrumming inside of me like a lilan's note, long and pure. I lay down on the floor in front of the warrior, and unfastened my dress from top to the bottom. It fell upon the floor beneath me, showing me to him like an unwrapped present.

He'd seen me naked in front of him before – but I'd never showed him that I was ready to be his Queen. Not like this.

I waved for his attention with the scepter, feeling silly and brave in equal measure, and then slowly brought the emerald bulb to my lips to feel its chill. Then I rolled it down, rubbing it against each of my nipples in turns, spinning it so that what was hot became cold, and what was cold became hot. My magic started growing inside my hips, that feeling of aching and longing that needed release.

I brought the gemstone up to my mouth and kissed it, taking it in, sucking on it, until it was warm and wet, and then I pushed it down to my own petals where Beza had rubbed me not long ago. The stone was smooth perfection and as I nudged myself with it my hips began to rock in arcane time. My magic moved inside of me and I moaned at feeling it, listening to the sound of my pleasure echo in the chamber.

I changed my grip on the scepter and pushed it lower, until it was nestled outside my soft place, and with a few smooth strokes I pushed it in. I startled at the cool straightness of the scepter's shaft, but my magic roiled again, and soon I stroked madly, half-lidded eyes looking up, imagining that it was *him*.

Yes – it was cold – but – I could – my magic – in my dark place – make it hot – and wake him. I closed my eyes tight and imagined his transformation as I rocked the emerald in and out, seeing him come to life, the color of his stone changing like the mountains at dawn, until he was leaning over me, taking me himself. The vision of it was so real that I didn't feel the scepter anymore or know it was my own hand, it was him, mounting me, thrusting, and I released with a soft shout, imaging him falling over me, a creature of flesh instead of stone, shouting himself in my ear, suffused with the power of my magic.

My magic curled me up again and again, pulsing through me until I collapsed, exhausted. I kept my eyes closed until it was finished, trying to write the future with my imagination, before I pulled the emerald out of my tightness with a low groan.

"And that's how I will wake you," I said, finally looking up. His countenance had not changed in the slightest. "And after that, they will take us off to another palace, where you and I will rule forever and a day, just like all the screens promise."

I smiled up at him and turned over to fall asleep on the floor under the ever-watchful eyes of my King.

2

_____

I woke inside the dream-cradle with a pain in my hip. Its walls were currently pulsing a pleasing shade of purple supposed to, I thought, entice me to stay inside of it longer. But every time I woke up inside of it, I was more tired than when I went in – I rose up and pushed the lid open, finding Joshan waiting right outside.

"To your bed, my Queen?" he suggested.

"Please." He reached in and swooped me up from the cradle, carrying me across the room to lie atop my bed – it was massive and had metal posters that rose up like trees with mechanical lilans nestled in all the branches to chime pretty songs. Despite my bed being bigger, the cradle out-massed it somehow, taking up one whole corner of my chamber, conduits snaking out of it in all directions, sinking into the floor and up into the ceiling. The cradle looked like a cocoon which, I supposed, made me its butterfly, only I never felt very pretty upon leaving it. It was right though, to sleep there – I was the Dream Queen, and sleeping in the cradle was how I fed the people of Aranda, with the essence of my dreams.

Except I hadn't been doing a very good job of it, if Mazaria was starving. I knew the feeding was metaphorical, though the spirit of the land was my spirit – it was yet another reason why I couldn't leave the palace. Secretly I chafed at the responsibility – and maybe that's why they were starving? Because I didn't give as freely of my love as I used to? I hoped not.

Joshan returned to my bedside, with the screen and scepter he'd found beside me in front of the Zaibann. "My Queen, would you like me to stay here?"

I – I didn't know what I wanted right now. But the pain in my hip persisted – I reached into my robes and found the strange object I'd rescued from the zoomer yesterday. Was it just yesterday? I looked at the pattern the light made on the walls – it was morning now, I'd been in the cradle overnight. Days inside the palace were hard to follow, and I needed to count them now, with Tide's Day coming – I pulled the object up and out and looked at it.

It looked...like a screen. Like a broken screen, one that only showed one page at a time. It took me a moment to realize what it was, my brain still slowed from the cradle – but I thought I held a book.

I showed it to Joshan. "Have you ever seen anything like this?"

He took it, inspected it, then gave it back. "Never, my Queen."

Neither had I. But I had read of them before, on screens, ironically. I flipped from page to page, looking to find meaning. I was sure it was covered in words from their placement, but none of them made any sense to me.

"Would you like food, my Queen?" Joshan offered.

"Please," I said, waving him away.

By the time he returned, I was no nearer understanding it but more certain that it was meant to be understood. No one would have taken so much time to draw so many symbols if they had no meaning – this wasn't a robe or a rug for mere adornment. Someone had hand-written this book with care, and if it was as old as the vase it'd been found in what kind of stories would it tell?

I wanted to know. I stared at the words, willing them to mean something to me, waiting for something in my mind to shift so that I could decipher them. When that didn't work I looked around the room for something, anything, that could help me, and Joshan walked in.

My servant set a tray of food on a nearby table and bowed before leaving again.

"Joshan – wait."

He wheeled on one heel, looking back. "Yes, my Queen?"

"Come here. Please."

He did as he was told, coming nearer. He was in his robes now, but I knew what he looked like out of them. I knew how strong his arms were when he carried me, and I knew how impossibly gentle he could be with his hands, even though they were twice the size of mine.

"I need your help, Joshan. Lay on my bed with me."

Without question, he lay beside me. I reached for his hand, bringing it to my lap and pushing it down. Layers of fabric kept him from actually touching me, which was fine – I wanted to access my magic, yes, but I wanted to keep it dulled enough to stretch it long.

"I need you to – yes –" I said, as he began to rub. Joshan always knew what best to do. And with him touching me at my brightest spot, my legs only open wide enough to let two of his fingers press, I held the book up and stared at it with intent.

My magic didn't take long to answer him. I could feel it being swirled up with each soft movement he made. I tried to channel it through myself, imagining myself able to read the strange words, summoning visions of light pouring out of my eyes and understanding pouring in.

But nothing happened. I closed my eyes in frustration and let myself move with Joshan instead, my hips rocking their own accord, wanting more than just his subtle touch – and when I opened my eyes again words flickered on the page.

"Stop," I commanded, pressing my hand on his forearm.

"My Queen," he said, and waited.

Long moments passed. The magic he'd coaxed up in me held, trembling inside with desire, but the words didn't change. Had I imagined things?

"Again – but, more slowly."

He stroked me again, his hand moving beneath mine, rubbing with soft gentle patience. We'd spent hours like this before, over the course of one day, him stoking the fires of my magic only to let the embers cool before stoking them again. It'd been a delicious torture, done as much for pleasure as just to see if we could, how long we could walk down this path together and me still stay Queenly and sane.

I breathed heavy and refocused on the words. "Come to me," I begged them. "Let my magic make me see."

My hips rose under Joshan's hand, my body begging for what my mouth wouldn't command, and he rubbed me harder but even more slowly. My breath caught and my eyes almost closed, tempted to end this experiment, throw the book across the room and command him to enter me – I knew he was ready, his hard cock pressed against my thigh – and as if he knew I thought on it, he pulsed his hips against me, one time.

"I want to know," I told the book and the powers hidden inside me. "I want to see." My free hand twisted lower to grab at him through the fabric of his robes, and he began to thrust into my hand. "Please," I begged the book, my slave, my magic. "Please –" I made the word into a hiss as my magic coiled, ready to spring, and I didn't have the self-control to order Joshan to stop. "Joshan –"

His hand rubbed me faster, knowing what I needed from frequent practice, and the bed bucked beneath us both as he thrust against me hard. "My Queen," he whispered, his breath hot in my ear as he answered me.

It was all I could do to hold the book up over us, as my body tensed, the full force of my magic coming on.

"I want to know!" I commanded, and then my magic was upon me. I screamed low to high as it raced through my entire body, emanating out, making me shake uncontrollably in its wake. Joshan still rubbed but his weight was against me, his hips thudding into my hand, his smooth cock stiffening until, with a helpless shout, he relented, following me.

I moaned. Somehow my free hand still held the book up and I looked at it with half-focused eyes, the end of my magic roaring in my ears, as I caught my breath from the force of its passage.

And when I next blinked – or the blink after that – or the blink after that – I could see.

The words on the page didn't change – but something inside my eyes did, so that I knew what they said. And I read, "The History of Queen Airelle," as clearly as if it were written on a screen.

"Joshan," I breathed.

"Yes, my Queen?"

"It worked – it worked!" I sat up in excitement, leaned over to kiss him joyfully, and moments after that I fell back to bed to begin to read.

I WAS RIGHT – it was a book, and I was proud that I had rescued it from the zoomer. I read through the night and up until dawn as the lilans chimed the passing hours outside.

It told the story of Airelle, a distant-distant Queen. Yzin had never mentioned her in history lessons – and despite the fact that the book purported to be her history, it was easier to believe that it was a convoluted work of fiction, or even a child's tale, because so much of the story was impossible to believe. She had magic that flowed out of her like fire – she was allowed to leave the palace – she was allowed to lead an army!

There had been no war on Aranda for thousands of years, but fighting seemed to be the only thing Airelle did – there were painstakingly drawn maps on multiple pages that explained where they were fighting, and then other pages explaining why, and how – with weapons I'd never heard of, men mounted on creatures I'd never seen in the Living Hall – the sheer imagination of it as a work was overwhelming.

Each battle was presented without comment, as though it happened every day, all the time. In fact, it seemed like the historian had gone out of his way to make such fascinating subjects dull – which, oddly, made it feel less like fiction as the story unfurled.

A pearl rolled in as I blinked dry eyes and looked up to see Joshan waiting hopefully. I rolled it back to him directly. "Play freely with one another, but leave me be."

He nodded at this, and set off to find Beza. Soon I heard the sound of their pleasure from not far away – it made me ache, but my curiosity to finish the strange story I was reading was stronger.

The fighting inside the book became more fierce. A distant country – Rix – joined the war from across the ocean, carrying weapons of metal that no one else could understand. The only thing that seemed to work against them was magic – but magic was in short supply. Airelle couldn't be on all borders, fighting all battles at once. She was exhausting herself, when her advisors came up with a desperate plan to close Aranda's borders with a shield from shore to shore. If they could manage that, they thought they would have a chance for their own technology to catch up to match the Rixans.

I slowed as well. Somehow I could believe that she could call storms from the heavens and fire from the wind – but put a shield over all of Aranda? I knew from my lessons Aranda was massive – it couldn't be done.

Her advisors spoke with her commanders – and the historian finally took the opportunity to describe one of them, briefly. I realized with a combination of excitement and horror that the fighters at the front of each of her battles, the creatures powered by smoke and magic and fierce loyalty – one of whom, if I read between the lines, it appeared that Airelle loved – were Zaibann. The shape of their armor – the way it was buckled – my jaw dropped. I got out of bed, and raced to my Zaibann's chamber to compare.

Everything the historian had written was accurate. His hair was back in a knot at his neck and walking around behind him as I had not done since he first arrived, I saw Airelle's symbol of the sun embossed on the stone armor covering his back.

Stunned, I raced back to my great chamber and threw myself into a couch, opening the book again.

"The dream-cradle waits, my Queen," Joshan said, bringing in a fresh tray of fruit.

"Not now, Joshan," I said, waving him off – and then I realized the irony of neglecting my people to read about a Queen who was prepared to give everything for hers. "Soon, though, I promise?" I amended. I was almost done, determined to finish reading quickly.

"Of course, my Queen." Joshan smiled and nodded, and I found my page before he left the room.

Airelle was quickly married to a Zaibann, Zaan, in an elaborate ceremony – elaborate not because of the cost or expense, but because of the magic involved – sealing her fate to his. I could tell throughout the course of the book – the history in it spanned at least ten years – that Airelle had always been closest with Zaan, of all her advisors, and the historian – if he could be believed! – was not shy about sharing that fact. He also did not back away either from their wedding night, saying in his dry way that the entire palace shook from the 'force of their bond'.

But mere days later, the real ceremony began. Whatever members of the army they could spare began digging a vast and deep hole. And when it was finished, the Zaibann flew into it, landing one-by-one, sitting in rows of a hundred men each. Airelle kissed Zaan, then stood on the edge of the excavation. She promised him – she promised all of them – that this wasn't 'a good-bye, but merely a parting'.

And then, through some combination of her personal power, mirrored and magnified through their own willingness to lend her theirs, the shield was cast – but at great cost. Because inside the pit, every single Zaibann in existence was turned to stone.

And that was the book's last page.

I twisted it, as though more pages might fall out if I shook it roughly.

"That's...all?"

I couldn't believe there wasn't more. It had felt so real it was like my life – it was better than my life, honestly. I was lost now that it was gone.

Joshan cleared his throat from the hallway. "If I may, my Queen?"

I looked up, and knew what he wanted. I didn't want to sleep now, but it was time. It was what Airelle would have done, if she were me. "Please, Joshan."

He crossed the room and lifted me, carrying me to the cradle and settling me gently inside before closing the lid. Its walls started to pulse in colors and I fell asleep inside the cradle with the book over my heart.

3

———

When I woke, I was exhausted. I peeked out, Joshan rescued me, and this time when he offered food I ate everything on the plate. The story I had finished was still rolling in my head just like the pearl – and I wanted to give chase.

I had to know if the book was real – or just another fiction with enough reality to give it bite. The easiest way would be to find the Chamber of the Zaibann with my own eyes. Not my Zaibann's chamber – but the one where he had come from, where the rest of them were stored. So when Beza returned to my room with a fresh dress for me, I sent her off to pack the three of us meals for our journey.

WE TRAVELED in silence down the longest of the halls. I usually told my slaves about the stories I'd read, sometimes even going so far as to read to them myself – but there was something about Airelle's that made me want to keep it hidden. It didn't feel like her story – it felt like it was mine.

Which was foolish, and I knew I only thought that because of how quickly I'd devoured the book. Still, though – we'd traveled an hour, me mostly lost in deep thought. I looked around to get my bearings, and found we were near the Map Room – and I had a sudden idea.

"Beza –" I grabbed her wrist and hauled her into the room. I'd been here before with Yzin, as he lovingly showed me maps of Aranda. It'd been deadly dull, I'd paid attention only to humor him, but now I knew what I was looking for.

I pushed wall after wall of plastiglass covered maps aside, centuries of Arandian history, until I reached the lowest, oldest, ones, where only fragments of their maps remained – and then I turned to my slave girl.

"Kiss me," I told her, and she nodded, agreeably.

She stepped forward and I wrapped my arms around her, pulling her into me with a fury I did not know I possessed, feeling her body pressed against mine. I felt my magic move inside me – restrained for days of reading and my time in the cradle, it was like a starving urshak, and I could feel it leap forward inside of me. I spun Beza so that she had her back to the map, and I opened my eyes as I ran my hand down the curve of her ass.

A flash of light – could the others see it, or was it only in my mind? – and then the words on the map reformed, just as the book's had.

I released Beza slowly. "My Queen," she whispered, touching her lips with one mystified hand.

"Thank you," I said, gently moving her out of the way to inspect the document.

NOTHING HAD CHANGED for either of them – they couldn't read, but they claimed the words still looked the same. After a few hours of willpower and kisses – and me sucking on Joshan's cock for a time – I felt heady with power, but I still had no direct proof that Airelle's story was real. Names were similar to the book on the ancient maps, but not precise. The contours of countries had changed with time, and over eons rivers had run dry – but I felt myself getting closer. In the same way that I could feel out the hidden pearl we played with, the one that's path led to magical things, I believed I could feel out the mystery of Airelle.

And so we left the map room, and continued down into the deep halls.

We walked for an entire day without pausing.

I knew it would be down here, somewhere – if I was going to believe any of the book's contents, all of it had to be accurate, and we were at the oldest part of the palace. Zoomers still patrolled down here, but even their endless polishing couldn't change the rough-hewn quality of the walls, or hide the increasing fragility of genuinely ancient art crumbling inside of equally decrepit frames.

This was where it had to be – the book had said the pit was deep, well, we were deep now – and it had to be big enough to hold five thousand men – well, the halls were further spaced, and all of the rooms here more wide.

I'd heard the story about the celestitians choosing my King my whole life, my one-out-of-five-thousand, but I'd never realized the history behind it before. All those Zaibann, trapped inside my palace, waiting endlessly in stone for a rescue that had never come.

I put the book under my arm, held Beza's hand on one side, Joshan's on the other, and closed my eyes. The truth was down here somewhere, all I had to do was find it – and I had help.

"Joshan, kiss her."

My slave stepped forward to do as he was told. I heard Beza's breath catch as he stepped close to her, pulling her in with his free hand. I imagined him holding her close, his cock rising between them hopefully. I remembered the way he'd tasted in my mouth yesterday, the sweet smell of him, and then other things too – what he could do to me, what he would do to Beza if I commanded him – I opened my eyes to see him merely kissing Beza, but still felt the sharp pain of being left out.

That was what I would draw on now. The statues, if they were here, had been denied for centuries. I would find them by their hunger.

I watched Beza tilt her head so that Joshan could taste the softness of her chin and neck, imagined his breath against my skin, her lips against mine – I felt my power roil in me, and sent it searching.

I stretched my powers thin, pushing through walls in all directions, felt as though I was combing through history itself. I heard Joshan and Beza, and let go of their hands as the sound of their kisses and rough breathing continued. I felt thinner and thinner still, spiraled out almost far enough that I wouldn't be able to pull myself together again. I reached my limit, I'd never sent so much of myself out before – and just as I tried to regroup, I felt a pull.

I stumbled to the right, following it until it faded, then looked back at my slaves, who were in the process of disrobing one another. Watching their skin revealed – Joshan's strong arms stroking across Beza's smooth back, the way his hands grasped at her hips, picking her up just as he'd picked me up before, to settle her darkness around his stiff cock. I gasped with the memories, and my powers rose inside me, pushing me toward a wall.

It was covered in artwork, portraits of people I didn't know – I swatted them aside, to clatter to the floor and fall into dust, but behind them, a sigil was revealed. The symbol of the sun – Airelle's symbol, representing the life she gave to her people.

The sun she lived under, that I had never seen.

I threw myself at the door, and to my surprise it gave.

I yelped at falling forward into blackness, then Joshan was there at my side catching me nakedly. "My Queen," he apologized, as he hauled me back.

"I'm –" I looked between him and Beza. I felt bad for interrupting them, but I couldn't stop, I was so close now – "The lights I asked you to bring, where are they?" He nodded and went to retrieve them, along with his clothing. Beza pinned her hair back up with a breathless grin, and I grinned back. If I was right, there would be release and rewards later, for everyone.

. . .

THE STAIRS SANK AND TURNED, sank and turned. No zoomers came down here, everything was covered in a thick layer of dust. I wondered darkly which councilman had had the honor of polishing my Zaibann's stone cock off before presenting him to me.

Then we turned again, and suddenly the chamber opened onto a wide pavilion full of armored statuary. Row upon row upon row of warriors. Every single remaining one of Airelle's Zaibann army.

I stood still for a moment, stunned.

"My Queen?" Joshan asked, looking from the statues back to me.

I ignored him and trotted the rest of the way forward. The light only illuminated the first ten rows or so, but every statue was different. The way they buckled their armor was slightly personalized, varying heights, a head cocked here, an arm raised there.

"Shine your light up," I said, and pointed. Joshan did so, and illuminated Airelle's sun symbol with rays blazing on one wall, just where the book had said it would be.

If they were here...then everything in the book was real. I looked down at my hands. I was a Queen too – so where was my power? I threw my arms wide in imitation of her, trying to call lightning down or fire but nothing answered me.

Up until now there'd been the chance that the book was a story, a child's tale, no, a perversion, a poisonous account from some cruel and enfeebled mind. But now that it was real and everything in it proven true I had no one to blame for my own weakness but me.

Beza stepped into my line of sight, looking up. "My Queen?" she said, with a note of concern.

"I'm fine, Beza," I told her, but my hands were still clenched into fists as I paced along the front-most row.

There was a gap in it, at the end. I could tell where Kings had been taken, to be married off to prior Queens. I pursed my lips – the stories I'd been given about ruling after my wedding ceremony were always so vague. I was told we'd go off and rule side-by-side in a new palace, even better than this one, but where that was or why we had to move or how we'd rule jointly, all of that was hidden from me. And any time I did ask, I was told that we would discover how to rule

together, that I shouldn't be constrained by rules from a prior time –
the discovery of my future was made to sound like a gift that it would
be a shame to open early.

Truth be told, it had been a long time since I'd asked the councilmembers because I knew they wouldn't tell me, and I hated feeling
just like this.

But – when I did have my King – things would change. We would
change them together. I was sure of it.

And I knew who I wanted for my King.

"Zaan –" I said aloud, and turned, as though one of the statues
would answer me. I flipped to the page in the book and reread it –
there was no indication of where he'd stood in line once he'd landed,
only that he was among their number. "Zaan? Zaan!"

He was still here, surely. I gathered my will and tried to send
power out, but felt nothing, just like earlier. "Joshan –" I said, and
snapped my fingers.

"Yes, my Queen?"

"Take me like you were taking Beza. Now."

He pulled his head back. "Of course, my Queen –" and leaned
forward to kiss me.

"No. Not that." I was too angry to wait. I just wanted power. I
grabbed my skirts. "Pick me up –" I commanded, and he did so. I
wrapped my legs around him. I finished pulling up the last of the
fabric separating me from him, and reached down to find his hard
cock lining up. I pushed his robes apart and brought him out,
fumbling in the tight space between us, until he was aligned with my
darkness and I was ready to settle on top of him.

"My Queen," he whispered, head bowed near my ear as I pulled
myself to him with my legs, pushing myself down.

His hands cradled my ass as he slid in, rough and slow. I panted
atop him, the desire for power flowing through me, replaced by
actual power as he and I locked, his cock deep inside. I groaned,
feeling the first wave of strength ready itself, my magic beginning to
form and coil.

He lifted me up and pulled me back down, again and again. My honey flowed freely and my voice rose as I called out for my power, Joshan taking me fiercely as I clung to him.

"Yes – Joshan –" I wound my hands into the fabric of his robes to hang on. He penetrated every bit of my darkness and my petals rubbed against him and – I twisted as the magic came over me, looking out at the statues, reaching toward them with one hand.

"Zaan – Zaan – Zaan –" I made his name into a cry while Joshan rocked me through release. I shuddered in his strong hands, my place squeezing against him all the while, taking the last of my pleasure as my power flowed out. "Zaan –" I whispered again, sagging down in Joshan's arms.

He held me there, as I sometimes asked him to after my time in the dream-cradle, until I could raise my head. "My Queen?" he asked. He was still hard inside me.

"Thank you, Joshan –" I said, unlacing my legs. He pushed me away from himself, and set me gently on the floor. I turned back to the wall of soldiers behind me. Not a one of them had moved – or if they had, I'd missed it.

I stood there, catching my breath, feeling realization settle. I was not Airelle. I was not even one tenth of her.

When I could talk again, I looked to my slaves. "Let us return."

Beza nodded, picked up the lights, and led our way back.

THE PASSAGE back to the familiar hallways near my great chamber was a painful one. How had Airelle had so much magic? Was it like a muscle that could be built up? Or had it, over the eons, been spilled out and lost? The council said my only magic was in my dreams, and they harvested those from me at night. But that wasn't right, I did have other ways – what if I confronted them and called them liars? What purpose would that serve, though?

All I needed to do was wait until Tide's Day, when the ceremony was complete. And then my King and I – but I couldn't finish the thought, because I realized despite all the stories I'd been told, I didn't really know. A deep weariness born of impotence and frustration settled over me – I felt as though I had emerged from the dream cradle again.

"My Queen?" Joshan asked, slowing as I had.

"I'm very tired, Joshan. Carry me?"

"Of course, my Queen," he agreed, and did so, so that I could close my eyes and try to sleep.

When I woke, I had been bathed and placed in fresh clothing and was lying on my bed with Beza waiting nearby.

"I'm fine, Beza," I said, answering her worried look. "Run along."

She curtsied and did as she was told.

One of them had placed the book beside me. I considered throwing it across the room. How come Airelle was so powerful when I was not? But it wasn't the book's fault that I couldn't live up to history. Why had no one ever told me of her? Or told me the truth of the Zaibann? Her story was my birthright – why had it been hidden from me? I rested a hand upon the book and had a strange feeling like someone was reaching through the pages to touch me back.

Was Zaan still below? Or had he been turned into some other Queen's King, and I'd missed my chance?

I quieted myself and clutched the book to my chest, and imagined everything the historian had reported of him – how the braid of his dark hair landed halfway down his back, his wise and piercing eyes, the tales of his strength in bed and in battle.

So much history, lost to time. What would he think of powerless me, now, were I to save him? Who knew. What would my own King think of me, whoever he was? I sat up in bed, determined to go ask him, even though he wouldn't answer.

I walked into the Zaibann's chamber, past the tables and benches that'd been placed there for our feast, right up to his statue.

"I know you can't hear me, really, but – while I am a Queen, I'm not Airelle." My eyes searched his face for softness or understanding, but only found his stern visage. "I don't have half the power she had – I promise if did, I'd turn you back now. I know you've waited long enough." I put a nervous hand on his strong stone arm, and remembered what the historian had written about Zaan carrying her off to bed their first night.

I stared up into his face in a way I hadn't dared before, trying to see who he really would be when I woke him. His chin was cleft and there was a small scar under his left eye – I reached up to stroke it with a tentative finger, and then pulled back. I'd left the book in my bedroom, but I knew what I'd read. It couldn't be – could it? I circled him, comparing notes from memory with what I saw, and soon I knew.

My King was Zaan.

I said his name aloud, while gently shaking him, as if I could wake him up. "Zaan." I rose up on my tip-toes to whisper it by his ear, "Zaan," while feeling his cock press against my thigh. That was the only thing the historian hadn't written about, I thought, looking down.

Airelle's magic was so much a part of her she never had to explain it. She beckoned and the world was set ablaze. But all my magic rose from deep inside. I wrapped a hand around his cock and felt my dark place ache.

He would be mine in time. All I had to do was wait until Tide's Day.

But I'd just promised him I'd free him – and before that, Airelle had, thousands of years ago.

I wanted to be like her, no, better than her – I wanted to be the kind of Queen who kept her promises.

And so I knelt down.

4

I took him into my mouth like I'd taken Joshan before. The smooth stone was as cold as I knew it would be, but I took as much of him in as I could, wrapping my lips around his shaft. I wouldn't have my servants' help now, all of the magic would have to come from me –

I sucked on him, stroking my tongue underneath his cock the way that Joshan liked. I acted as though everything were real, imagining it inside my own mind, until I could see it as it should be – my King, standing above me, thrusting, taking my mouth to pleasure himself. When the picture in my mind was perfect, I pulled back, looking up. He'd warmed up so much inside my mouth that I was disappointed to find all of him still stone.

"Wait," I told him, as though he might escape me. And then I scanned the room – there was a chair with a high back nearby. I ran off to pull it nearer, deafened by the sound of it dragging across the floor, until it was close enough for me to utilize.

There was no choir and it was no wedding ceremony but it would have to do. I disrobed and arranged myself in front of him, then was daunted by the thought of what I was doing, so I turned around so I wouldn't see. I grabbed hold of the back of the chair, spread my knees wide, and slowly lowered my hips down, preparing to take him in.

His stone cock nudged against my folded flower, and I was glad for the spit I'd left behind as I pressed back. Joshan had taken me like this before, but his cock wasn't as full or as relentlessly stiff. I slid on and off what I could take of him, slowly taking his cock deeper as my honey smoothed the path, glad my mouth had made him warm, using my whole body to ride. My nipples brushed against the back of the bench, tightening as his cock pressed in, inch by inch.

"Please – Zaan –" I began. He was my King, and I would call him by his name. "Please –" I begged the stone to penetrate me, to let me cover him, and then – I found myself flush against him with a moan. I trembled, at feeling him deep inside, and with the delicious perversion of doing such an unceremonial act.

My King, however, was unmoved – but I didn't feel my magic flowing in me yet, either. And I wouldn't until – I balanced one hand between my breasts on the back of the bench, and slid the other between my legs to press against my folds as I continued to rise up and down, pulling off of him and then taking him back in. In moments, my power began to gather, and I imagined myself like Airelle, strong and powerful and one with him. I thought of what it must have been like on their wedding night, if he mounted her like this – of how I would feel when he would mount me. Heat flowed out from between my legs where stone met flesh, my fingers were slick with honey at imagining him behind me, whole, his hands grasping my waist, pulling me in him with as much strength as I needed him – my darkness tightened as my magic did, both wrapping around the smooth stone, readying, taking him tight – "Zaan," I warned him before my release, in case stone ears could hear. "Zaan!"

I shouted his name as my magic shook through me, making me shudder, pinned by his cock. I tried to focus it on him, into making him whole, but there was too much – I could feel it spill off of me like water over the edge of a pool. It roiled through my body and I had no control over it as it endlessly spilled out.

"Zaan," I whispered his name now, feeling his stone cock still hard inside me. Whatever I'd done, whatever small powers I'd had, hadn't been enough.

And then strange hands grabbed my hips. "Airelle," he moaned, and started stroking of his own accord.

I stiffened for a moment, afraid to look back and break the spell, and as he thrust again I moaned. My King was taking my dark place, as the celestitians had ordained – and nothing had ever felt so right. I felt my magic surge again at being stoked by him, ready to release a second time, and my hands held the back of the bench tightly.

His heat covered me from behind as he leaned over and pushed my hair away from my neck. "I see you've misplaced your collar," he rumbled low.

"Collar?" I answered, feeling my magic ready to explode.

There was the chill of his buckles as they pressed into the naked skin of my back, the warmth of his presence, and then the heat of his breath as his mouth lowered onto my neck – yes – one kiss from him and my magic would –

He bit me. Hard.

"Zaan!" I jumped forward and the chair almost toppled, as I rolled away from him, holding one hand to my neck, hearing myself scream. He was behind me now – an actual Zaibann, no longer stone – and looking at me through blinking eyes, with a deepening frown, his lips colored by my blood. He took a step nearer and I kicked away from him, getting up to run.

"Who are you?" he asked.

"I am Queen Ilylle!" I shouted, feeling my blood seep through my fingertips.

There was utter horror on his face at that moment – and then Joshan tackled him.

They went to the ground together, my King and my slave. "Joshan, no!" But before I could call my servant back, Zaan had thrown him across the room. He looked to one side and spit out – saliva still tainted by my blood, I could see it on the pale stone – and then made to go after Joshan again.

"Zaan – don't!"

He stopped, his hands reaching for weapons that hadn't made it through time with him, though their scabbards were still hanging from his hips, and he whirled on me. "How do you know my name? Where is this place? Where's Airelle?"

I stood up, shaky and still naked. Beza rushed in, holding up my dress for modesty. I took it with a bloodstained hand. "I will answer your questions. But attack no one else."

"My willingness to attack depends entirely on what your answers are."

I swallowed and nodded, as Beza fastened my dress around me. "You are the Zaibann warrior Zaan, consort of Queen Airelle." At my giving his name and rank he nodded subtly. "And I know that because I read of you in a book."

At that, his eyebrows rose and he laughed, a harsh sound, perhaps part of his throat was still stone. "I had no doubt they'd write of my exploits someday, girl, but it's a little too soon for that." Then he looked around the unfamiliar room again and his expression darkened. "Where is this? And where's Airelle?"

"This," I said slowly, trying to placate him as though I were in the same cage as a jacar, "is the Feather Palace. It is where I am Queen – Queen Ilylle, Queen of Dreams."

"And Airelle?" he demanded, stepping forward.

"Has been dead for quite some time."

He stood so still at that, that I would have believed him stone anew. "Impossible."

"I am sorry, but it is true."

"No –" he looked around the room for exits. "I refuse to believe."

There seemed no point in fighting him.

"This is some ploy from the Rix. They sent you to me, to bind me to you –" he spat again, and this time his spit was clear. "Otherwise, why would I be fucking you?"

I didn't know the word, but I felt safe assuming what he meant. "That...was me. I needed to do it, to access my magic, to wake you."

"Fucking isn't magic, girl," he said and advanced a step. "Take me to Airelle, or risk losing your life."

The enormity of my mistake settled on me. How impetuous I'd been to rush into waking him, just to see if I could compare. For him, everything in the book had happened moments ago – not eons.

"I would, if I could, but she's dead."

"Who killed her?"

I shook my head as he took another threatening step. "I don't know."

"Someone killed her. Or she would have released me."

Beza, bless her, had been clinging to me but put herself between us, whereas Joshan, finally recovered, started to move to intercept. I flung my arm out to keep Joshan back. Zaan was my King, I couldn't let my servants hurt him, or vice versa.

Zaan's breath came hard. "Who killed her?"

"I don't know." How I wished the book had gone on for just a few more pages!

"The greatest Queen Aranda has ever known did not just die."

I took a step free from Beza and Joshan and did quick math from my history lessons with Yzin. "It has been twenty-thousand years since you were turned to stone, my King. No one lives that long, not even royalty."

His eyes narrowed and there was another long, stone-like, pause. "That I would even entertain your suggestion is absurd. There's no way so much time has passed. If it had, would we be able to still understand each other?"

"I have a gift with tongues, my King."

"And my brothers? Where are they?"

"Still stone, row-upon-row. I can show them to you, if you like."

He paused again. Emotions crashed across his face – so much anger, fear, and pain – and the historian's book had said nothing about how much of him you could read in his eyes. "I am sorry, my King. I wish I had thought about what it would be like for you when I woke you, I truly do."

"I don't want your pity," he said low, and jerked his chin. "Are you holding me hostage?"

I shook my head quickly. "No, of course not."

"Then I am going," he said, and stalked out.

IN ALL THE stories I had ever read on screens, Kings always stayed with their Queens, willingly, in love forever inside their palace. I knew those stories were childish now, but I had no idea the reality would be quite so cruel. Maybe the ceremony I'd skipped was necessary to tame him? Blood seeped from the wound on my neck and a trail of it stained the edge of my dress. None of the stories had ever mentioned biting. After a moment I ran after him and found him standing in the nearest nexus, unsure which way to go.

"You bit me –" I told him, from a safe distance.

"Yes, I did. Where is the door?"

I blinked. There was only one door that I knew of, the door of the council chamber. How would that look, for me to take him there? Then everyone would know what I had done, what I'd ruined with my impatience. I clenched my hands into fists – I only had myself to blame.

"It's this way, my King," I said, and started walking on the council's path.

He followed beside me at his own distance, Joshan and Beza close behind.

"If twenty-thousand years have gone by, why would you still call me that? Surely I am King no more." His voice was flat and measured, as if he knew catching me in a lie wouldn't change the truth.

"Because I am a Queen, and every Queen has a King chosen for her. There's supposed to be a ceremony. A choir." Like mentioning it now would change what had happened. "And then, because of my magic, you wake up."

"Awakened by the magic of your pussy?" He sounded incredulous, and I looked down, feeling myself blush. The word he used for my dark place was strange, but I knew what he meant when I heard it.

"Yes. That."

He snorted and walked faster, as if he knew the path – then

stopped at the next warren of halls. I noticed him looking around, at the caged lilans, the unfamiliar sculptures and portraits, and could almost sense the otherness radiating off of him.

And I wasn't the only one. A zoomer walked up – and he kicked it aside. It landed on its back, all eight mechanical legs futilely swimming through the air.

"Don't!" I shouted as he went to step on it.

"It's Rix-made!" Zaan seemed to flicker in front of me as he shouted.

I put myself in his path again, pressing an earnest hand to my chest. "It's only a zoomer. It cleans the halls here."

"It's Rixan," he snarled.

"No one even knows what Rix is anymore. Or where it is. Or if it ever was. I only know because of the book."

The zoomer flipped itself right and crawled back over. Dusting implements unfolded from its feet and it began combing over nearby tiles, coming closer before turning to crawl down a different hall.

He watched it and then looked around, taking everything in, me, the palace, my servants, the lilans, and shuddered. "This – this place – everything about here – is wrong."

"I know it is all different for you, and I'm sorry," I said, nodding deeply before gesturing. "Come this way, my King – we are close to the door."

WHEN WE REACHED the council chamber, I took him inside. Stalactites pulsed overhead, going from cheerful yellow to a golden green, while the screens lining the far wall showed a pleasant picture of the Arandan countryside. Zaan stopped, looked around warily, and then walked over to them.

"Windows?" he asked, trying to push his hand through the nearest one. The image flickered, becoming fertile crops on rolling hills, and he jumped back. "What magic is this?"

"It isn't. These are screens. They show my people and my lands." This, I was proud to show him at least – he ruled them too, didn't he?

"See the mountains of Nestri? The port of Isoto? The palace, from the outside, when the sessest are in bloom –" I named the images as Yzin had taught me until they repeated themselves and Zaan watched them with a furrowed brow.

For one sharp moment I felt like this must be what it was like to have a King at my side. Then he stepped back, shaking his head. "Where is the door?"

I pointed. It was set into the chamber's far wall, as tall as the ceiling and inset with jewels. He ran over to it, searching for a handle with his hands, then finally throwing himself into it bodily, but it didn't move.

"What kind of joke is this?" He whirled on me, his braid whipping behind him.

I shook my head. "It isn't a joke. That is the door." It was the only way I had seen anyone enter or leave the Feather Palace for my three hundred years – and suddenly I understood his problem. "It only opens from the other side."

He made a strangled sound, then hit the door with both his hands. When he left the room this time, I did not chase after him.

5

Twenty-thousand years.

I had never heard anything so absurd, not even in the stories the *varjans* told me as a child. Who was that woman, and why did she look so much like Airelle?

My footsteps echoed in the empty hallways that seemed to never end. Would I have to count out twenty-thousand steps before I found an escape from this accursed place?

There had to be a way.

I stalked down halls, looking for doors or windows, waiting to feel a swirl of fresh air. Any window I did see was an accursed Rix-made screen – I took great pleasure pulling these off of walls, but there were no windows hiding behind them, either.

What hell was this that I was trapped in? And how could I get out?

I found a place where animals were all in cages. Some of them I recognized – the number of feet were the same, though the markings on hides and feathers different – but there were others I'd never seen. I stood outside the cage for one of these. It had fangs as long as my hand and a body that wove sinuously through the brush of its habitat. I paced outside its range, a double series of bars keeping me from it and likewise, and felt it stalking me as tried to think.

That girl who called herself a Queen – hardly. She had none of Airelle's fire or strength. I had watched Airelle tame and ride a *raguin* in one afternoon, without magic. If that girl saw a *raguin*, she would faint, and then the *raguin* would eat her.

I and my mean were only meant to be stone for a season, or at most, a year. Until our spies had figured out how to make Rix-machines work for us. It was never meant to be an eternity.

I put a hand to my mouth, where that strange girl's blood was still on my lips. No matter how quickly I'd tried to spit it out, I'd swallowed some of it.

She did wake me. And now I was bound by her blood, not the blood of my beloved.

I whirled and beat my hands on the nearest bars. "Airelle!"

The creature inside the cage took its chance, flinging itself at me claws out, mouth open, and rebounded off the cage the same as I did.

"Airelle!" I shouted again, as if shouting could erase the passage of time and bring her back.

The growling of the beast inside the cage was the only thing that answered.

I RETURNED with Joshan and Beza to my chambers. Beza looked up at my neck. "May I bathe you, my Queen?"

I touched my neck and flaked off drying blood. "Please."

Together, we walked to the pool. Usually, baths were a time for silliness and merriment and kisses on wet skin. Today, however, I was in no mood. I settled into the water and swam back and forth.

I would have to call and tell the council – I already knew Railan would be upset, and Yzin, and all the other councilmembers, and even unknown, unmet celestitians. I'd ruined everything. I supposed the only thing left to figure out is if things could be fixed.

I rose out of the water and let Beza towel me off, then sat down so that she could stroke a comb through my long hair. Her comb stuttered, so unlike her that I looked up. "What are you thinking?"

"I am afraid if he lays down to sleep, the zoomers will get to him, my Queen."

I snorted. "After twenty-thousand years, I don't think he'll be sleeping for a very long time."

Some Queen I'd become, maddening my King and losing him in the palace. I touched the spot on my neck where he had bitten me – wild with anger, surely. It was healing – the few times I had ever been injured, those injures never lasted long – but the wound to my pride remained.

Beza was closing the fastens on a fresh new dress, when Joshan came in. "The King has returned."

"He has?" Perhaps he had found his patience displayed in a case in an unexplored hallway.

Joshan nodded. "Yes, my Queen. And he states he is hungry."

I watched my lips twist to one side in the mirror, as Beza tugged my wet hair up and set it with jeweled combs. "Hopefully he doesn't want to eat me, again. Set us a table – and I will join him shortly."

I WALKED into the dining room with Beza by my side. We only used it for ceremonies, the rare times when the council came and ate with me inside the palace, but it felt right to use it now with him.

"My King," I said and bowed.

His eyes flickered over me and there was something in his face like surprise. "Impostor," he acknowledged me. I stood quietly, chin up.

"Are you going to bite me again?"

One eyebrow arched and the corner of his lips pulled up into a sneer, showing the sharp tip of one fang. "No."

"Good," I said, and took my seat right by his side.

Joshan brought out the first course and I noticed Zaan watching to make sure I ate things first.

"Nothing is poisoned."

His eyes narrowed. "How would a caged creature like you know of poisons?"

"I've read stories," I said, thanking Yzin for every screen he'd ever brought me.

Zaan grunted. "I shouldn't be worried about dying anyhow. Clearly I'm already in Draugulos." He looked at me for a response and when I gave none, he continued. "A place of eternal torment for Zaibann who have lost their way."

I nodded. I'd never heard of it before – but I'd known what it was when he'd said it. My magic was still at my side. "There is nothing that can torment you here. The Feather Palace is designed only for pleasure."

He looked at me with great sorrow in his eyes. "Do you know what would please me?"

I shook my head and held my breath in foolish hope.

"The return of my past, my people, and twenty-thousand years."

"I am sorry." I stared into my soup. "Does that mean you believe me now?"

He ignored my question. "I want to see the book."

I looked over to Joshan, waiting in the doorway. "Please, Joshan, retrieve it."

BEZA BROUGHT our next course out and we ate in silence until Joshan's return. He handed the book over and I passed it to Zaan. He took it from me without question and began to read.

"Rkatrayzin. I would recognize his handwriting anywhere. The historian, eh? More like the man who was merely there."

He started reading faster, skipping pages, until he got to the end and our dinner was cold. "There are no answers here," he said, throwing it across the table.

"I never said there were."

He shook his head again, as though he could negate the ages. "I cannot believe that so much time has passed – not until I see it for myself. Take me outside, immediately."

"It...is not allowed."

The look he gave me then – I wished that I had sat across the table from him, or in another room entirely. "What kind of Queen hides inside her palace?" he asked me.

"The lives of all Aranda depend on me," I said – the same answer Railan had always given me. I wonder if it tasted as bitter on his tongue as it did mine.

"Airelle would never let herself be caged."

"She let you be caged, didn't she?" I said. Zaan's face flushed and I instantly regretted it. "I'm sorry –"

His hand lunged over and grabbed my wrist tight. Joshan started toward us but I shook my head. "Show me your powers, girl. Show me some lick of her strength."

I tried to wrestle my hand back from him – only getting it when he let go, and he laughed cruelly.

"You have nothing. You are nothing, compared to her."

"Don't you think I know that? I read everything –" I rubbed my wrist with my other hand. "But I want to be like her – and you're the only link I have."

"Then show me your powers," he challenged again.

I looked down at my wrist where his fingerprints showed. "I can read ancient things."

"A librarian. How quaint." He pushed his chair back from the table. "Anything else? Anything more?"

I swallowed and inhaled. "When – I released you. That's when I have powers."

There was silence while he stared at me. "You mean fucking, girl? You're only magical when you fuck?" He made a gesture in front of me, and I knew what it was – a dark place being pierced by a cock.

"Yes. I am magical when I...fuck," I said, trying out the strange word. "It worked with you, didn't it?"

"Don't expect me to thank you, waking me up to the loss of my love and the betrayal of my entire kind."

"Look – just –" I pulled my chair next to his. "If you want to see what I can do," I put my hand over into his lap, wondering if he'd grab at me again, finding the folds in his clothing that would let my hand in. "Let me show you."

His eyes lowered and his jaw clenched – but inside the circle of my fingers, I felt his cock stir.

6

My head ached from the impossibility of it – and because every time I looked away from her, she looked like *her*, my Airelle. It was as though someone had painted Airelle, and someone had then painted that painting, and then again and again – I knew it wasn't her, and yet if my eyes were half-closed or she were only seen out of the corner of my eye, I hoped.

We were bloodbound, she was beautiful, and I hated her.

And then she pushed her slender pale hand beneath the black leather of my armor and took hold of my soft cock.

"You hope to enspell me?"

She smiled placatingly. "You wanted to see my magic – and I wanted to show you."

She stroked me as any temple whore could have done – was she as innocent as she seemed? How could anyone be so naive? If it had been anyone else doing what she did to me now – I would have cut their hand off and fed it to them.

But I didn't stop her because she did look like Airelle. My Airelle never would have spoken so quietly or put up with my bursts of anger, but her fingers wrapped me and my body answered. She wasn't *her*, but she smelled the same, and if I closed my eyes –

"See?" she said, as I stiffened in her hand.

"You ruin it when you speak," I growled, and she shut up – but her hand didn't slow.

She played up and down me, her hand like Airelle's, skillful, deft. But Airelle would have had her other hand in my hair, wound tight, making me beg her for release, praying for a drop of blood. At the memories of so many nights lost with her, exchanging pain for pleasure, my cock swelled, and the hand stroking it pulled faster in response.

I took hold of the edge of the table and came with a groan, imagining Airelle at my side, my Queen the temptress, always taunting, teasing, driving me mad – and I inhaled deeply, praying that by the time I exhaled circumstances would have changed.

But no, when I opened my eyes I saw her there, staring at the lacy wetness of my seed in her palm.

"What happened? Have I hurt you?" She showed her hand to me.

The spell – such as it was – was broken, and I was disgusted with myself for my hope.

"You have made me come, my Queen." Another thing to hate her for.

"But Joshan –" she looked to her male servant and then again to me. "He doesn't leak."

I looked to the man in the doorway. He was as tall as I was, all muscle bound, watching what happened without comment – without jealousy. "You've fucked him? And he's never spilled seed inside you before?"

She shook her head.

More Rix-sorcery.

I took my head and put it in between my hands, elbows on the table. I really was in Draugulos. I must have dishonored myself somehow. I started laughing harshly. "They're not real."

The girl looked from me to her servant. "What are you saying?"

"They're not real! None of this is!" I stood, throwing the table across the room, foodstuffs sloshing onto the ground. "You, thing, come with me." I grabbed hold of the servant girl's waist and hauled her aloft. "I don't know what kind of demon puppet you are, but I intend to find out."

THIS WASN'T how I thought things would go at all.

"Stop that! Come back here at once!" I shouted at my King – and he completely ignored me.

No one had ever done that before.

I stood still for a second, befuddled, and then chased after him so quickly my seat tipped back and fell over. "What are you going to do with her? Where are you going?" He'd slung Beza over one shoulder, her hair dragging along the ground behind her like a trail of blood.

"If what you say is true, I have twenty-thousand years to catch up on. I'll be starting with her. And if I am in Draugulos, my actions have no consequence, for I am already doomed."

I ran around to stand in front of him. "You are my King! I demand you act like one!"

His eyes narrowed. "I've never met a King before. How ought I to act?"

And my children's tales betrayed me. "I – I – I don't know."

Zaan sidestepped me and kept walking, and stopped when we reached a chamber with a wide couch. He threw Beza down on it and she bounced on the cushions.

"She's not real. None of this is real."

"She is too real. You are – aren't you Beza?"

Beza looked up at me. "I am real, my Queen," she answered, without any fear in her voice.

If I were in Beza's position, I would be horrified. A gnawing fear started in my stomach and I put my hands there, wiping Zaan's seed off on my dress. If he was right – what did that mean for me? For everything I ever knew?

Zaan stood in front of her, unbuckling his armor. He pulled his chest piece off, and took off the robe beneath it, revealing a broad, muscular, scar-covered back.

Who had ever whipped a King? I put my hand to my mouth to hold back a gasp – and then ran around to put myself in front of Beza. "I don't care. She's real to me. I won't let you hurt her."

He set his folded robe on the ground near his armor and then looked at me, his braid trailing over one shoulder now.

"I thought you would be different. The stories say we're King and Queen of Aranda and we live happily ever after."

He snorted in disgust. "Are all the books you read child's tales?"

"No." I quickly shook my head. Some of the books Yzin had been bringing me lately were quite grim – though not as frightening as unleashing my own angry Zaibann. "But the ones that ones that mention you and me are," I said. "So I'm sorry that I don't know how you ought to be – but I know that you shouldn't do this."

He stood in front of me, breathing deeply. Zaan was everything I thought he'd be from reading the book, but a hundred times more frightening than I could have ever fathomed. He looked down at Beza again, still prone on the couch where he'd dropped her – she hadn't even tried to run away.

"She's not real. I don't smell any blood in her."

"Neither do I!" I agreed, even though I didn't know what blood smelled like. "But her dark place drips honey, same as mine –"

"Dark place?" he said, eyebrows rising, eyes focusing in on me.

"Be-between her legs. Her pussy." I used the word that he'd used for it earlier.

"You've tasted your own slave?" he asked, his lips quirking up.

I nodded hesitantly.

"But this is the only one you have, right?"

I nodded again, wondering how he knew, as he began to shake his head. "No real woman tastes of sweets. Men only say they do to please them."

"But she does," I protested.

Zaan smiled wickedly. "Shall I see?" He sat down on the far end of the couch. "Come here, slavegirl."

Beza looked from me to him and I didn't know what to say.

"Your King commands it," Zaan said, his eyes looking at me. At that, Beza did as she was told, crawling nearer, and Zaan pulled her onto his lap.

I realized his skin was against her back, and he wrapped her with one arm. Since I had released him from the stone, I had only felt one small part of him, no more. I was worried for her, but as he brought his other hand up to brush the fabric covering her breast, I also found myself becoming jealous.

He pushed Beza's hair out of his way so that he could press his face into her neck. One hand kept stroking her breast, as the other met her thigh. "Are you scared, my darling?"

Beza shook her head, "No, my King."

Zaan glanced up at me to make sure that I was listening. Then he murmured something just for her and rocked back, pulling her with him, kissing her neck.

I almost said something then, worried that he would bite her – just as I felt my magic stir inside at watching them.

She writhed against him, falling back into him like I had seen her fall back into Joshan a hundred times before, raising her arms up so that she could reach for his face and hair. She ground her body against his, as he kissed and licked and nuzzled her, his hand massaging the weight of her breast, his hand on her thigh ever-rising.

"You are warm, for a demon-puppet," he said, licking a stripe up her neck to whisper in her ear. His hand on her legs reached her hip and then slid over to dive between her thighs, and she moaned as I could only imagine him pushing a finger inside. Her eyes closed and I watched his arm move as he stirred himself into her, feeling her slick heat. And when he pulled his hand out he brought his fingers to his lips and tasted her with a cruel smile.

"Honey indeed."

He stood, pushing her roughly aside, walking across the room to me. I held my ground. I could smell her scent on him – I'd been intoxicated by it before.

"Be honest – does the same drip from between your legs? Or do you own the wetness of a real woman?" He stood an arm's length away and then reached over to smear her juices on my cheek. I stood there, furious at him. If Beza wasn't real, then what else about my life was lie? What, if anything, was truth?

Zaan pressed on. "Did you slick honey on my cock? Are you made of candy, girl?"

I shook my head, staring hate at him. "No."

He nodded his head with a tilt. "Because no woman alive tastes like that." He cast a glance back to Beza who was innocently looking from him to me. "Shall I wrench her arm off to prove to you she's not real?"

"No!" I ran across the room and grabbed Beza's wrist and hauled her to me. Even if she wasn't real – she was still my servant. "You are my King. If there is to be – fucking – then it should be with me."

Zaan crossed the distance between us and I fought not to shrink back. "Trust that there will be," he said, burning me with his gaze, his eyes running over me like hands. "But not tonight. Leave me. Have the male bring me beer if the world still has it."

He took a step back and I hauled Beza out of the room behind me.

I PULLED Beza all the way back to my own sleeping chamber. I had never needed doors before, but now I wished I had them, so I could close them and bar the path. I did not want the Zaibann startling me in the middle of the night.

I sat on the edge of my bed, hands in impotent fists. "He is awful," I told Beza. Staring into her eyes now, though, I knew what Zaan had said was true. She was kind and loyal, but not any more human than the zoomers that smoothed the rugs at night.

"He is your King, my Queen," Beza said innocently.

"Leave me," I said, and she turned to do as I commanded. "But do not go to him, nor let him touch you."

"My Queen," she said nodding, then left.

I WATCHED HER GO, pulling the Rix-abomination behind her. What had happened to this world in my long absence?

I had to admit that it was long, now. Unless this entire palace was some sort of elaborate trap.

But if so – why that girl?

She was a pale shadow of Airelle and I was bound to her by blood. She clearly didn't know what the binding was – I needed more power over her before she did. Something to trade.

I needed a way out.

One of the accursed metal creatures raced by me on all eight legs, and I turned to follow it.

IT WALKED DOWN ENDLESS HALLS, through open doors, past others of its kind, scrubbing things clean, trimming living branches, grooming caged beasts, until it reached a wall with a handspan gap at the bottom. I watched in amazement as it folded itself down, lowering until it could slide sideways and duck underneath, like an insect scurrying from a sudden light.

Well, well.

I sat down. Airelle and the pathetic impostor weren't the only ones with powers. I placed my hands in my lap and called on my magic, speaking the meditative words in the old tongue.

"Zaibann are creatures of the wind. We come and go as we please, and no man can halt our passage."

I felt the pieces of myself lighten and pull apart. I occupied the same space that I had before, but I was as air now, a cloud-like consciousness controlled only through sheer force of mind.

I sank, collapsing in on myself in a smoke, and followed the metal-thing out.

THE TUNNELS I was in as a mist were as extensive as the ones I had walked in earlier. The metal – how I hated being encased in it! – threaded through the walls so that the Rix-creatures could bring in supplies and haul out waste. I knew the Chamber of the Sun my men and I had dug was set inside deep stone, so any time a tunnel branched, I lifted up. The entire system couldn't be perfectly sealed – if it was, that sad girl and her machinated friends would have suffocated, not to mention all the animals.

I rose, conscious of how much time it was taking me, and how much of my strength I was using, knowing I would need enough strength to go back – and I cursed myself for waking with such ravenous need, never thinking that I might be tricked. My anger made me vibrate, so much so that I almost missed it – the wafting of a faint breeze.

I pushed myself toward it and hovered right in front of the draft. There was always the chance I could be dissipated so much that I could never reassemble, so I waited, testing cautiously, until I found a gap between the metal panels and leaked ever so slowly outside.

I reassembled my form on the edge of a metal shell – there was no need to waste my powers more than I had, not when my body could heal quickly – and I slid down, tumbling along the shell's edge for what seemed like miles before I dropped to the ground.

The fall was long enough that even I was stunned upon landing, and when I caught my breath the air tasted like ash. Like after the battle of Hotalle, when Airelle lit up the city's walls and the fires smoked for weeks.

Draugulos indeed.

I looked around. It was night, but the area around me was lit with an unearthly glow. Whose magic was this that illuminated me? Surely not *hers*. I saw lights that weren't flames atop poles – more Rix-made abominations.

Then I heard a sound from behind. I turned as a loud creature raced straight at me on two wheels, ridden by a hidden man in armor. He shouted something, muffled by his helmet, and veered around. I stood there, feeling the wind from his passage.

The things we had fought – the things my men died for – they were everywhere.

Was our entire war for nothing? Had my slumber been in vain?

I stalked away from the palace's metal wall, looking for darkness to hide in.

I WALKED DOWN long alleys that stank of refuse and defecation. There were no pictures of this place on the palace's screens – was all Aranda like this, now? I passed doors that held back sounds of people and music like I had never heard, walked over men sleeping in small groups wearing shreds of clothing, too inebriated to feel rats nipping at their fingers.

Lights flickered on a wider boulevard ahead – as much as I hated Rixan objects, I flew towards them like a moth.

What had happened to the world? And why didn't that girl inside the palace know? What was the point of keeping her so innocent – and who gained from keeping her trapped there?

I looked up and couldn't see any stars. Had the world lost those, too, while I slept?

I heard a sound from close behind me – scurrying feet. Like a rat, but man-sized. I turned.

"Give me all your money."

I had no idea what he was saying, but he brandished what I was sure was a weapon. Twenty-thousand years and some things will never change.

"Come on! Give me all your money!" he said. I stepped closer to him and he stepped back, holding the weapon up higher. "I mean it – I'll cut you – I'll –"

"I am Zaan the Fearless and you will regret this decision."

A second later he was slashing his knife through the air where I used to be. He shouted, more words, it didn't matter – I reached in and grabbed hold of his shoulder, while he tried to slash me through. I made the parts of myself in his path smoke and so he stabbed nothing. Avoiding his blows was second-nature – my scars were from training, not battle. I hoisted him up, and his shouts turned to screams as his weapon clattered to the ground.

I held him there as he howled. If I spoke his language, I knew I could have asked him anything – but where would I even begin? How much time has passed? Have you heard of a Zaibann? The name Airelle, is it familiar to you? I clenched his shoulder tighter and tighter, hearing bones pop, the unanswered fury of twenty-thousand years pouring out of me, until urine trickled down his leg. I set him down in disgust, and his hand found something in a pocket and threw it at me. I caught it, releasing him, and he ran off cursing.

The thing he'd thrown – I opened it up. Inside were cards I didn't recognize the use for – and one piece of paper that I did. I smeared it with some of his blood in pulling it out.

It had her face on it. Ilylle's.

The sky was getting lighter – dawn was coming. While the world would be less frightening in daylight to the people that lived here, I would become moreso. I walked back to the palace wall, changed into smoke again, and wafted the piece of paper back up with me on the wind.

I TOSSED and turned that night. Nightmares about creatures of stone, and people in the screens, beating on the glass, trying to get out – it was a good thing I wasn't in the dream cradle, or I might have poisoned my people. When I woke, Joshan was there.

"Queen Ilylle, your King appears to have left."

I lay back exhaustedly. Did I have to tell anyone? Perhaps the celestitians could choose another Zaibann for me – but what if all of them were like him?

"Is there anything I can do for you, my Queen?" Joshan asked, worry creasing his brow.

I looked up at him. He, like Beza, was just an elaborate zoomer – four limbs, instead of eight. No wonder he always knew the time – or when the Council called. He was a lie. Everything in the palace a lie except for me.

No, not even except for me. I was a lie too – ruling a people I never saw, lands I'd never walked. There was no proof that I was a Queen. For all I knew, the palace and everything in it could be a dream. And one of my titles was Queen of Dreams, wasn't it?

I felt like I had dove too deeply into my pool and stayed down too long, like I was running out of air. I felt my throat close, my heart race, no matter that I was lying in my bed. I had never felt this way before – it felt like I was dying and I looked to Joshan.

"Come here and hold me," I commanded, and when he was prone beside me, I looped my arms around his neck and cried.

I MUST HAVE FALLEN ASLEEP AGAIN – I didn't remember, but when I woke up the pulsing lights of the dream cradle were all around me. I stayed inside it, curled up, unwilling to face the rest of the palace again – until I heard the sound of someone pacing back and forth outside. I pushed the lid open and the pacing stopped – I saw black leather boots leading to black pants and armor and finally Zaan, staring down inquisitively.

"Your servant told me waking you would be harmful," he said, pushing the door up, squatting on his heels. "What is this contraption?"

"It harvests my dreams. It is how I help keep Aranda safe and well," I told him, even as the words tasted bitter on my tongue.

He looked at me and one of his eyebrows rose. I avoided his gaze and he snorted softly. "You do not believe in yourself as much as you did yesterday, do you."

I swallowed and didn't answer him.

"I have good news for you then," he said, rocking back up. "You actually are a Queen."

"Of course I am," I said, with more conviction than I felt. "But –"

He held up a piece of paper – and I realized with awe that it had my likeness on it. "What is that? Is that...currency?"

His dark eyes studied me. "You have never seen its like before?"

"Never."

I gathered myself up inside the cradle and stood, stepping out of it. But between my weariness and my skirt catching, I tripped. He caught me effortlessly, then picked me up out of the chamber and set me down.

"Do you have you your footing?" he said, without kindness.

"Yes," I said, as he released me. I carefully walked over to my bed and prayed he wouldn't follow too closely. "The paper – please –"

He handed it over to me and it was my face. The same one I saw in the mirror each morning when Beza dressed me. I was printed in a shining blue and there was a smudged thumbprint on the corner – the same color as blood.

"Did you steal this?"

Zaan shrugged. "I wasn't injured. He survived."

"You –" I looked from the paper to him. "You injured one of my people?"

"Do you care so strongly about a public you have never met?"

"Of course I do! I'm their Queen!" I showed him the paper as though it were proof. "They rely on me!"

"For what, precisely?" he asked, his tone cold.

I gathered myself and swallowed before answering. "I dream their dreams. And – Railan has me read things, sometimes, so that they can hear my voice. And," I waved the paper in front of him, "this is currency. They honor me. They value me. Should I not do the same for them?"

I sat on the edge of my bed, staring at my picture on the paper – and then realized the question I should have asked all along.

"How did you get out?"

Instead of answering me, Zaan asked another question. "In your stories, what happens to your Kings?"

"It is as I told you – King and Queen rule side by side."

He shook his head once. "No man could be content to be so trapped here."

I looked up at him, fury burning inside. "What about Queens? Do

I seem content to you?" I rose to standing and willed my magic to catch him alight, only it wouldn't answer me. "How did you get out? Tell me. I want to see the land I rule – I want to meet my people."

He leaned back, the corners of his lips subtly rising. "Make me tell you."

7

I knew from my brief time outside why they kept her in here like a songbird. She wouldn't last a minute outside in the brutal world I'd seen. And her powers – if she could be said to have any – were so weak as to be almost useless.

Which was perfect for me.

I could take all the blood from her I wanted, and no one would ever find out. I imagined myself swelling up like a tick – until she died and I died with her.

Bloodbinding was inherently unfair.

I rocked back in the chair I sat in, waiting for her to do something foolish to attempt to seduce me, to use her 'magic' to bend me to her will. Instead she sat back on the bed and looked at me hard, as though she were memorizing my face and said, "Tell me about Airelle."

I stared back at her, challengingly.

"The book is all I know of her," she pressed.

I shook my head. Airelle was mine – she was still alive for me, not just words inside some book. And if I deigned to tell her, where would I begin? How the dawn looked, reflected in Airelle's eyes? The way she could best a man in battle? How the *ozri* drifted down to sing for her? How when she swam a river, scaled *garmanders* swam at her side?

A thousand-thousand memories rushed to the surface for my attention, as the little impostor stood.

"I know I am but a poor copy of her – a copy of a copy of a copy. But something in me is still the same. I do have power. And I know from reading that book the lengths she would go to for her people. I would do the same for mine."

Her hands went to the fastens on the front of her dress and unclasped them. It fell from her in a rush of blue – how had the printers of her currency known that that was her best shade? – and she stepped out of it like a *phine* leaping out of ocean foam.

And for a moment, she looked like *her*, truly – her skin shining white, her straight blonde hair falling to lap around all her curves and edges. A creature of will and desire – and power. I felt it pull at me, like a whispered word, like a gentle hand. Nothing like Airelle's commanding presence, but – I closed my eyes to shut her out.

Whether I liked it or not we were bonded.

"Put your dress back on. We have things to discuss."

I WAITED until I heard the first fasten click shut. "What do you know of my kind?"

"Only what I have been told." She looked shyly over at me, through a rippling wave of hair. "That you are a Zaibann, destined to be my King. From the council, the celestitians, and the children's stories that you mocked."

"And what do you know of blood?"

"I...have cut myself before." She sat back on her bed now, watching me with caution.

So much innocence. It was both alluring and repulsive. I wanted to smother it with blackness, to change her, to punish her as it seemed I had been – and I wanted to shelter her forever from the world outside. I was like a starved artist finding a uniquely perfect white dove – I didn't know if I should set her free, or eat her alive.

"Zaibann are priests of blood and smoke." I held up my hand in front of her and let it dissipate – her jaw dropped in surprise. I reformed my hand and laced my fingers together in my lap.

"That is how you got out, isn't it."

"Precisely. I followed one of your accursed metal beasts and found a route."

Her face sank. "Which means I cannot follow."

"Not that way, no."

"Could Airelle?"

I shook my head. "She was not Zaibann. Not even a Queen can manage what we do. We are born to it and then trained."

"My stories never mentioned that. The history did – but I didn't want to believe it." Her hand went to her neck, where my bite was already healed. "And nothing ever mentioned biting."

"When one is a creature of smoke long enough, you need an anchor to bind you to this world."

I watched her swallow. "Were you bound to Airelle?"

"No." She blinked, and I went on. "She wouldn't let me. When you are tied by blood –" My voice faded. How often had I asked her for her blood? How often had I begged? Of course the first thing I wanted upon waking was her.

But she knew as Queen that she might die – and she wouldn't see me fade.

"She wore a collar at all times. It was a symbol of her defiance."

"Should I withhold my blood from you, then?" Ilylle said, attempting to take a regal tone.

"You wouldn't be able to if you tried." I looked over at her, so small upon her bed, and saw her frowning furiously. My impotent, impostor songbird – something like pity for her moved in my heart. "But were you able to, I would die," I answered honestly.

She inhaled in a gasp. "Really?"

"Yes. *To taste someone's blood is to begin to die.*" I said the second phrase in the old tongue, surprised to see her nod as though she'd understood.

I expected some change to come over her at my revelation, a realization of the power she now held over me, some latent cruelty to shine through, but instead she leaned forward, her expression one of genuine curiosity.

"How often do you need it? And how much?"

"Once a day, and it depends." I touched my tongue to the tips of my fangs. It had almost been a day, now, and I had traveled very far as smoke.

She took several long breaths and I could tell she was thinking. "So when I woke you and I was collarless – you thought that I was her, granting you permission to take blood?"

"Indeed."

"And now you are bound to me? You need my blood?"

"Yes."

"Why didn't you tell me this earlier?" she asked, and then drew her lips into a straight line. "Because you did not believe me, until you went outside."

I nodded.

"What is it like?"

Her eyes on me then – they were beautiful and serious. Blue as the dress she'd worn, as the money her image was embossed on. "It is very different from my time."

"Of course," she said, relaxing a little, giving me a soft smile. "But is it good? Are people happy?"

"I do not believe that happiness is a good thing, in and of itself. Pleasure must always be earned." On that, Airelle agreed with me.

Ilylle frowned. "Are they...earning it? Or are things too soft? Like – in here?"

"No." How to tell her that the pictures her screens showed her were false? That the first thing a man from her time had done was try to rob me?

She read the truth in my eyes and sank back. "It isn't like the screens show, is it."

"As Queen, you should know the truth – the air over your land tastes like ash, and your streets smell like a sewer." She shuddered bodily as I told her, like my words were blows. "Your people – the ones I saw were fighting one another, or being gnawed upon by rats."

Her hand went to her mouth in horror. "It's just like the screens –"

"I tell you, it's not –"

"No – the ones Yzin brings." She leaned over the edge of her bed and held up a stack of thin metal. "The stories in them. They're so dark. Bad things happen all the time. But I always thought everything in them was made up. Just stories." She looked over at me. "Same as you."

I shrugged.

"Is the...whole world like that? All of Aranda?"

"I do not know."

"What have I done to it?"

I leaned forward and put my elbows on my knees, piercing her with an intentionally cruel stare. "You have done nothing. Which is almost as bad a crime as doing evil itself."

She swayed on the edge of her bed, looking around the confines of her room. I may have lost twenty-thousand years, but she had lost her sense of self. I wasn't sure which of us was currently poorer.

Her mouth opened and closed several times as she sought out the right words. "How can I fix it?"

"Become a Queen. A real Queen." I stood and crossed the room to her. "You need me as badly as I need you. Without your powers, you will never leave this palace, girl."

She straightened, attempting to be stern. "I am three hundred years old – my name is Ilylle."

"I am twenty-thousand, or so you say, and I will call you what I like." I leaned forward and took her chin in one hand. "You will give me blood and I will teach you how to use your magic as Airelle did."

She stared up at me, her expression defiant, scared, aroused. "Must there always be biting?"

"Not always." Then I smiled down at her so that my fangs would show. "But often."

As he stood smiling down, I was conscious of the way he loomed, and the fact that him standing and me sitting put my mouth on a level with his unseen cock. He let go of my chin, stepping back, and I swallowed.

"When should our lessons begin?"

"Now. Tell your beasts of metal and unreal creatures not to intervene."

While my servants were not in my room, I knew they were always listening. "Joshan, Beza – no matter what I say, leave the two of us alone for an hour." An hour was long enough for one lesson, wasn't it?

Zaan smirked. "Will they hear you?"

"They always have before."

"Good. Stand."

I did as I was told, not knowing what would come next.

"Take off your dress," he commanded.

I put my hand back to the fastens and paused. It felt like my dress was my last piece of protection – or would be, until I learned how to use my powers. How cruel that I could only access them without it. I started opening the fastens slowly.

His eyes flickered to my hands and then back to my gaze. "I won't kill you – killing you would kill me."

My fingers stopped. "But you admit you mean me harm."

"Your powers will never arise without it. Others learn to fight against their siblings as children, or parents – the push and pull of growing up. But as you have none – and I doubt anyone inside this palace has ever told you no – you never had will to push against, remaining ignorant. And the servant that you've fucked – you never got any true power from him, because he doesn't know what it is to be powerful. He would never fight back." He reached out a hand for the bottom set of fastens. "I, on the other hand –" he began, and jerked me toward him. I gasped as the last set of fastens fell free inside his hand, and reached to catch my dress as it dropped to my hips.

"Your life has been too easy, walking listlessly from room to room, watching caged jacars." The word he used for them was strange, but I knew what he meant. "Reading stories you didn't even think were real – not knowing what was happening right outside your door." He stood so close, looking down at me, no matter how many times Joshan or Beza had seen me naked, I'd never felt so exposed before. "I have to baptize you in reality, girl. It will not be my fault if it feels like drowning."

I nodded, not daring to look up, and felt his hands upon my hips as he threw me onto my bed.

Zaan crawled up after me, armor and all. My heart leapt into my throat and started fluttering. His armor pressed against me and a knee slid between my legs and I thought I would feel him in my dark place, my pussy, but no – he rose above me, knees on either side of my hips, straddling me trapped between his thighs. His eyes wandered over my body and I almost wished that he'd touch me instead of using his calculated stare, looking down as if he were seeing through me, until he finally spoke.

"The first time you felt your power – tell me about it."

I inhaled, then looked away, suffused with an unfamiliar feeling – shame. Yes, this was definitely shame, from what I'd read about it before – Zaan leaned forward and took my left nipple between thumb and forefinger and pinched it, hard. I gasped and looked up at him.

"That hurts!"

"I know," he growled. "Tell me your story."

"It was in front of you!" I confessed, but the pinch didn't stop. I breathed through the pain and went on quickly.

"It was after the celestitians chose you and had the zoomers bring you up. There was a feast, all the councilmembers came, and their wives and servants – everyone was happy. Happy to be there, and happy for me. It wasn't until afterwards that I had time alone with you, to see your face.

"I –" It felt weird telling him this story – how I'd looked at him, trying to figure out what kind of man he'd be. "I just wanted to know who you were."

One of his eyebrows rose but he didn't say anything.

"I'd never seen a Zaibann before. And – I'd never seen a cock."

"How did you learn its name then?"

"Joshan." I felt myself flush red. "I – he caught me looking at yours. I said it seemed silly and he said that it was not." It was unlike Joshan to disagree with me – that was the first time he ever had. "And I asked how he knew and he said that he had one too. I commanded him to show it to me – and when he did, when it was hard, I knew where it must go."

Zaan made a low sound, and reached into the plackets of his armor with his free hand, without letting go of me. "Go on."

"I told him to lay down on the ground, on the floor in your chamber. I straddled him, much like you're straddling me now, and I moved my skirts aside, sitting slowly down, until his cock pressed against the entrance of my dark place –"

"Your pussy, girl, get it right," Zaan said, pulling his own cock out to stroke in front of me.

"My pussy," I corrected, watching his hand move. "I took him inside me, slowly at first, then faster and harder, and then he moved beneath me, too." I remembered that it felt so good I'd wondered aloud if it was right. Faithful Joshan had told me, "You are the Queen. All rights are yours," without missing a single thrust.

"And that was when it started?" Zaan asked, one hand still pinching me, the other calmly stroking himself.

"Yes. I could feel it then. Gathering inside of me. In my hips. Pulling in and coiling tight, getting ready to release." I grew breathless at the memory. "I rode him and he rubbed places that I never knew inside of me, like we were locked together in a dance that I didn't want to end." I looked up at Zaan, I could feel my power gathering again underneath the weight of him. I wanted to touch myself – I wanted him to touch me. I wanted him to take his hard cock and push it into all the places Joshan had ever touched and more.

"Go on," Zaan said, his voice rough.

"And then my magic exploded." I moved my hips below his in imitation of the moment, begging for his cock, but the stern expression on his face did not change. "I felt it roll through me, blinding me with power." My hand came up to cup the breast he didn't pinch, pulling at my other nipple. "And I knew then that I was meant for something more."

He released the nipple he held and I hissed aloud in pain, as blood ran back in, reviving angry nerves. At that, stroked himself in earnest, until his hips thrust and he gave a low groan, his seed shooting out of his cock to spill across my stomach.

I lay beneath him, panting – unsure what I was prepared for, but knowing that I was ready. He smeared his seed up my chest and neck with one hand, and pressed two fingers into my mouth, pulling my jaw open as he stared down. Then with a grunt he released me and dismounted, stepping off of the bed and leaving me behind, naked and stained. He was walking toward the open hallway.

"Zaan – wait –" I sat up, throwing an arm across my breasts. "What happened? Was that...okay?"

"I don't know," he answered. "Was it?"

I looked down at myself, I could still feel the heat of him, and I was still wracked with need, my magic surging in me, unanswered. "No. It's not. What about me?"

"What about you?" A cruel smile lit his face. "Did you want something more?"

I opened my mouth, afraid to say what I wanted – then my anger made me bold. "I wanted to be taken."

He laughed, a harsh sound in my quiet chamber. "You will have to learn to take what you want, girl – or learn to live with what you're given. Consider that your first lesson, I'll be back later for your blood," he said, and left the room.

I sank back onto my bed, my dark place aching, my mind utterly confused.

8

I tried to make sense of things and then I started feeling sticky – I stood and walked to my bathing pool, where Beza met me and washed away his seed without asking any questions. I wanted to tell her what had happened, but what would be the point? She wouldn't understand.

So I swam laps and thought. What would he do next? Was he lying about teaching me? What could he teach me, treating me like that? I put a hand to my nipple underneath the water. It still stung.

I rose out of the pool with more questions than answers, and ate bites of fruit as Beza dried me off. When she was done, Joshan appeared in the doorway.

"Councilmember Yzin is here to see you, my Queen."

I froze. Where was Zaan? If Yzin saw there was no statue – "Take him to my chambers, and keep Zaan out."

"Yes, my Queen," he bowed, and left to do as he was told as I snatched a fresh dress out of Beza's hands and yanked it on.

BY COMING in the council door and going directly to my chambers, Yzin wouldn't see the empty room further down the hall. But I hadn't told Joshan to block Zaan bodily, and if he wandered – I flew down the halls, running into my great chamber at full tilt to find Yzin calmly sitting on my couch.

"Councilman Yzin –"

"My Queen!" He stood due to politeness, and at my apparent alarm, he looked behind me for a threat. "Is all well?"

I took in the room. Zaan wasn't in sight and Yzin did not seem displeased. "Everything's fine," I said, with a calm smile, giving him a gentle curtsy. "I was only excited to see you. I get so few visitors."

"I am sorry for that, my Queen. I have been overly busy of late."

"Of course," I agreed, and sat down casually across from him. "And the matter with Mazaria? Is that cleared up?"

I watched him carefully. He hesitated for a moment and glanced away before answering, "Yes."

I could hardly call him a liar without any proof otherwise, could I? And all avenues to get proof were closed to me. "Good," I said, with a tight smile. "So why have you come?"

He pulled a shard of pottery out of his pocket. "You gave me this."

"Ah, yes." I took it back from him, rolling it against my palm. "Is it special in any way?"

Yzin looked from the shard to me. "Only due to its age. It appears to have come from a very old vase. Maybe one of the oldest in your collection."

"I'm sorry we broke it then."

"Was there anything else strange about it?" Yzin asked, his shaggy brow raised high.

I suddenly felt guilty – or maybe afraid. Yzin had always been a mentor to me and it was his screens that first told me the truth – but I was still trapped in here, while he was free to go. What was the point of him telling me about the outside world if I would never live in it? Was my life just a game?

He continued solemnly. "Sometimes the artwork on the sides of old pottery tells a story. And sometimes, there are stories on the inside, too."

I froze. Did he mean the book? How could he possibly know

about it? I opened my mouth to ask him, and then saw Zaan in the hallway door at Yzin's back. I begged him to leave with my eyes, then smiled graciously at my councilman.

"I haven't had a chance to read your latest screen yet, Yzin," I confessed. "You know I do love stories, though."

Yzin leaned back, the moment between us lost. "It was a trait I tried to cultivate in you."

"And I appreciate that," I said as he rocked to standing, his knees creaking again. "Will I see you again before Tide's Day?"

"I would like that. Have Joshan call me when you've finished your latest screen."

"I will." I stood and followed him to the hall, only relaxing when I saw Zaan was gone. "Thank you for coming all this way. I know the stairs must be hard on your knees."

"I would climb a mountain of stairs for you, Ilylle," he said, turning towards me. Then he gently caught my head in his hands and kissed my forehead, before walking down the hall.

My impostor did have magic in her.

I felt it as I sat astride her, stroking myself to the words of her tale, her will gathering and searching out for obstacles to push against.

I could have done anything to her then, I knew from the way she ground against me in her need, the breathiness of her voice as she spoke, but it was more entertaining to watch her lose herself as my seed spattered her, and then be denied.

I wanted to deny her something. To take something away from her, as so much had been taken away from me. And then walk away from her bed with strength so that she would never know how badly I needed her blood.

None of the stories I'd heard of the bloodbound made it sound like this – I pressed a fist into my stomach where I felt hollow. To deny yourself too long was to become ravenous – Zaibann had accidentally slaughtered the ones they'd loved before, the warning stories were passed down every generation.

I was not there yet, but – I swallowed and found an empty room to lie down in, trying to maintain control.

I WAITED FOR HOURS, seeing how far I could push myself, needing to prove to myself that our bloodbond was real. When I couldn't take it any longer I stood, ready to walk into her chambers and demand it from her – but I was surprised by the sense of someone else's magic in the air. I dampened my own powers and crept up to find Ilylle talking to another man. A real man – I could tell by his scent. And when he stood, I was surprised to find him wearing clothes from my time, not what I'd seen men wearing outdoors.

Who was he, and how had he gotten here? He radiated power – and when she saw me, she looked afraid. When the man made to leave I ignored my hunger and followed him.

HE WENT to the chamber she'd taken me to with the false pictures on the walls. The sealed doors there opened for him and I turned to smoke to billow out before they closed again. We were in a hallway, with images of outside – just as false – projecting the top of a wide stair, but the actual door was set inside the screens to the left.

I followed him into a large room where embroidered robes hung from the walls and gilded hats and sashes sat on shelves – all styles of clothing from my time, but made in this one. He took off all his clothing and carefully hung it up, slipped on a uniform of some kind. A new door opened for him and he walked out.

We went through halls and doors, until we reached men, military in appearance, who stood at attention as he passed. Eventually he reached a final non-descript door, which let us out of the compound. Sunlight shone down through billows of smoke and the air around me still tasted like death. He walked carefully down three steps and into the belly of a waiting Rix-beast. I slid in right beside him, unseen.

"Were you successful?" asked a woman sitting in front of him, after he closed the beast's door.

The old man shook his head. "No."

"I'm sorry," she said, looking back at him in a mirror.

"Not as sorry as I am," he said, looking over his shoulder at the dome hiding the Feather Palace behind him.

"Not as sorry as she'll be, either," said the woman, with a dour face.

"Take me home, Elissa," the man commanded.

I wanted to go 'home' with him – I wanted to reform and ask him more – what did he mean? What did they know, that Ilylle didn't?

Did they plot to harm Ilylle?

I may have had no love lost for the girl, but we were bloodbound – I couldn't let her die.

The painful sinking sensation of need followed me, even as smoke – hunger, and fear, that something was transpiring to hurt her in the palace right now, without my protection. I needed to be able to find him again, but the old man had magic, he would notice if I marked him. The woman, however, would not. I swirled up through the metal-beast, catching a wisp of the woman's scent and tracing her with my gift, before exiting the monster's metal side via a puckered seam.

IT WAS easy to disguise myself as smoke in new-Aranda – no one would notice it, not with everything else already in the air. The slums were no prettier in the daylight as I flew around the palace to use the exit I'd used as wind. Inside again, I sank and turned until I was in the palace and blew through the halls to reform behind Ilylle, ready to demand her blood.

She was sitting at a desk, head bent, reading some Rix-screen intently. Her hair had parted, showing the fragile whiteness of her neck, and already I could feel the way my teeth would press upon it, the way it would give and then – my ravenous hunger frightened me, and I went still.

"I am returned," I said.

My words startled her. She jumped, clutching a hand to her chest as she looked back. "Oh – it's you. That was Yzin earlier –"

"I need your blood." Explanations could come later – I needed to feed now.

She set her screen down and loosely crossed her arms. "I don't feel like I learned anything this afternoon."

"Nevertheless, I need your blood." She had so many soft places visible, arm, breast, neck. Things low inside of me were aching, starved. "It is up to you if you give it willingly," I warned.

Her lips pursed and she snorted softly before standing up. "I've it given some thought. As I do get visitors sometimes, I don't want you biting me where it will show." She put her right leg up on the chair she had been sitting on. "Come here, my starving King," she said, and pulled her skirts up to show me her inner thigh.

I paused, even after seeing so much pale white flesh. What she wanted would put her over me, would give her a frisson of control. My pride didn't like that – but wasn't that what she needed to learn, rather than offering me a dainty wrist?

I needed to decide before my hunger made an animal of me. I swooped forward as smoke and reformed at her side.

She gasped, as I sank onto my knees in front of her. I wanted to be in control but failing that, I would take what was mine. I grabbed her leg with one hand and her ass with the other and opened my mouth wide, biting into the sweetness of her inner thigh.

She made a small sound of pain as I bit down. Her blood flowed, thick, sluggish, salty, and I looked up as I tasted it, surprised to find her staring down, eyes-wide and jaw-dropped. I ran my tongue against her thigh and sucked, pulling at the wound I'd made for more, as she slowly lowered one hand to rest against my cheek.

When I was sated – when the feeling inside my stomach was full, and sanity retook my mind – I closed my eyes and pulled back, and her hand followed me.

"Does my blood please you, my King?" she asked as I stood.

I wanted to tell her it tasted like treachery, like poison. There was only one person's blood I should ever know the taste of and that was Airelle's. But looking down at her, I found that I couldn't lie. "It does."

"Good," she said, and fainted.

I WOKE to someone smacking my ass – hard. I jumped and startled to all fours, finding myself on my bed and Zaan there, hitting me.

"What?" I asked in panic.

"You fainted. I assumed you didn't want me to slap your face, 'where someone might see'," he said, clearly mocking me.

The last thing I remembered was looking down at him, watching him suck on me and feeling...ecstatic. Wave after wave, feeling his tongue roll against me and his lips suck. I'd reached for his face, wanting to pull his mouth towards my honey –

"Are you afraid of blood, girl? Or did my visage frighten you?"

His voice interrupted my memories. "No." His lips were stained red – with my own blood. And I could see streaks on a pillow, likely where he'd cleaned himself so as not to scare me. "It wasn't that. I just –" I shook my head, unable to explain.

"Airelle never fainted."

"Airelle never let you bleed her, either." At least I had one thing up on my ancestor. His face flushed dark, and he stood to pace.

"That man who was in here with you. Who was he?"

"Councilmember Yzin." I looked over and saw the shard of pottery where I'd left it, on the couch. He'd been trying to tell me something, hadn't he?

"He's going to kill you," Zaan said, coming to a stop.

"What?"

"I followed him outside and got into a contraption with him. Heard him talking over a plan with an enemy."

"Yzin wouldn't –"

"You can't honestly report on what anyone *would*, my Queen. May I remind you your whole world is built on lies?"

"But he's the one who brings me screens. The screens that've been telling me the truth, all these years." I'd started reading the newest one immediately after his departure. And approaching it like history instead of fairy tales made all the stories in it much more grim.

"I'm going back outside, I need more information." He turned and strode away.

"Wait!" I jumped off the bed and ran after him. "How did you understand him?"

"What?"

"You heard what he was saying. Was he speaking your old tongue?" I watched my Zaibann's brow furrow in displeasure. "I did that. I told you I was good with languages. My magic – changed you." I poked at his armored chest with a finger. "Me."

"Perhaps you did. But it will take more than linguistic tricks to change Aranda – and in the meantime, if he kills you, he kills me. While you may trust him with your life, I do not trust him with mine." He pointed back at the couch. "Read your screens. See if you can find any answers in them. I'll be back before the end of the night."

And he changed right in front of me, becoming a twist of smoke that disappeared.

"Don't hurt him, Zaan!" I shouted, without knowing if he heard.

I LIMPED BACK to the couch and hauled up my skirts as I sat down. People in stories had injuries for days – years – while the bite on my thigh was almost healed, all I could see of it were the imprints of his teeth. My magic must make me heal quickly.

I rubbed at the streaks of blood his attention had left behind. What was it about his communion with me that had set me off? The pain of the bite, the indecency of the place, or the way his eyes were on me as he looked up and I knew that I was feeding him, like my blood was some rare elixir? I closed my eyes, trying to find that moment again inside me, but was unable to tease it out.

Opening them again – he'd set me a task to do, and I would do it. For my King, I thought sarcastically as I reached for my screen, and hoped I would find something in the story to exonerate Yzin.

THE STORY in this book was dry and cruel. A handful of persecuted rebels fought their government at great cost. So many deaths. Each one made me cry, now that I realized they weren't just characters in a book but actual lives lost, fighting my council – and by extension, fighting me.

But then the book changed tone, and became like the stories of my childhood. The few rebels that remained weren't fighting the government anymore – they were attempting to free a precious jewel from an evil magician's grasp. They had infiltrated the palace – a palace not unlike my own, I realized with some pain – but couldn't find it anywhere.

And that was where it ended.

There were pages and pages of blank space at the end without words.

The screens never had blank space at the end before – I traced my fingers over the space where words should be. Why didn't the story have an ending?

Because whoever had been writing it didn't know how it would go. I sank back with the weight of my realization.

"Food, my Queen?" Joshan asked, appearing at my side.

"Yes," I nodded absently, still staring at the screen. "And – bring me a pen and some paper."

9

L ike called to like the second I was outside the palace's walls. The portion of my power that I'd left behind on the councilman's servant as smoke – it pulled at me now, drawing the rest of me toward it.

I flew through the gray air, surprised that the city beneath me did not get any kinder. Rix-beasts moved on roads, but they didn't interact with the people on the street, who appeared bent by the burdens they carried on their backs, haggling with one another frequently. No one smiled, there were no emotions at all, except for bouts of shouting when enemies met – and everyone seemed everyone else's enemy.

I knew I was near her as the pulling sensation increased, but I was surprised that the area I was in wasn't any nicer. Surely a councilman, of such power as I'd felt, would live somewhere cleaner than here – did servants not live with their masters anymore?

But the sensation of pulling took me up the side of a building a hundred stories high, until I was looking into a window – my magic had found the woman, though we were separated by glass. She held a screen in her lap, and was staring at it intently. I quickly rose until I found a way into the building on the roof, and then sank down until I reached her door.

"Got it." She was talking to someone I couldn't see. Telepathy was an advanced skill, how had I not – no, she held some other Rix-made device in her hand.

I slunk up the wall so that I could see what she did. The thing in her lap had an image of Ilylle, talking. "I promise you that supplies are being sent. Be patient, and know that I think of you."

"See?" the woman said to an unknown someone. I wished I knew who was listening in. "It's clear she doesn't know what's going on. She's innocent. There's still a chance." She paused to listen – how? – tilting her head to one side. "I know, I know, but he says we must try. The worm nears completion. We've got five days at least, the high councilman cannot speed up the sun."

Five days.

I was tempted to reform. It would be easy enough to torture her into telling me what I wanted – but she was my only connection to the plot. I marked her room same as I had marked her, and flew back out.

I REFORMED the second my feet hit the floor of the palace. I'd been smoke for hours – longer than I'd ever managed to be smoke before. Another gift from Ilylle's magic? Or strength given to me by her sweet blood? ·

I stalked down the halls, thinking of the moment my fangs had pierced her thighs. The way her flesh was firm, then yielded, the salty-sweetness of the red that'd run out. An unfamiliar need washed over me, from the pit of my stomach to an ache in my loins – I was hungry. For her.

I walked into her chamber and she wasn't on the bed – but the lid to that dream-contraption was closed. Disregarding Joshan's warning, I lifted it up.

Ilylle was sleeping peacefully inside. The walls were pulsing in different soothing shades, and she lay on one side, her blonde hair spilled in a pool around her, lips softly open, eyes restfully closed.

She was beautiful. Not like Airelle was, but to deny it would have made me a liar. She was like an exquisite shell washed ashore after a storm, or the blooming of a single, perfect, orchid – and I wanted her to service every part of me.

"Ilylle, wake," I commanded. When she didn't stir, I reached in to shake her – and felt like my hand was burning off.

I yanked back and looked at my hand, front and back. There were no marks or redness on it, but the pain – I'd never been subjected to pain like that before. "Ilylle," I said with more warning. "Ilylle!"

It was like she couldn't hear me. I tried again, moving fast, to shove my arm in and out so that I could tap her – and again, the sensation of burning, plus a lessening of myself. I frowned and leaned over, looking around the inside of the thing, and I turned the tip of my forefinger to smoke. I dabbed it in, and it was pulled from me, lost. I sat back in wonder as I reformed it from other parts of me.

If the Rix-abomination had eaten my magic, what was it doing to Ilylle?

I ran for a table and dashed it on the tiles until I had a stick long enough to reach in and poke her. "Ilylle!" I shouted, hoping she'd wake up.

Her eyes blinked open and the colors inside the thing stopped. "Zaan?"

I tapped a hand inside and felt no pain. The horror was turned off. "Ilylle –" I lunged for her and pulled her up to me. "Are you okay?"

"Of course I am. Just tired. What's wrong?" she struggled lightly against me and I put her down behind me, afraid that thing would grow legs like the zoomers, cross the room, and attack.

"You can never go in there again." I took up another piece of the table and advanced, prepared to destroy the thing.

"Zaan – you can't – my people –"

"There is a reason you are weak my Queen – that beast's been stealing your magic from you."

"That's absurd."

I wished now I hadn't healed myself, so I could show her. "I opened it and it tried to pull my magic off of me." I turned and saw her leaning against the edge of her couch until she sat down, like an elderly matron. "Look how tired it makes you. Did you ever wonder why?"

"Because I'm servicing my people," she said, and then looked to me for hopeful confirmation. When I couldn't give her any, her head bowed and her shoulders slumped. "You mean this is a lie, too? I feel like such a fool."

I dropped the table leg and it clattered at my feet. "You didn't know any better. You've been doing the best you could with what you had." The depth of the treachery she was lost in was astounding. I wondered at the cruelty of men who would trap her here with their lies, and then harvest her magic off of her like they were milking some cow. Where did it go and what did they do with it?

Ilylle sobbed quietly, her head in her hands, and it was my turn to feel impotent. I stroked her back carefully, unfamiliar with being kind. "Just think how strong your powers will be now, if you never go in there again."

She looked up at me, tears brimming in her eyes. "But I have to go in, Zaan – if I don't, they'll know. They know when I go too long without using it. And they'll keep stealing it from me, and I'll never be strong."

My beautiful poor impostor. Emotions warred with logic warred with history as I stared down at the trembling curve of her lips. "I know one way your magic may be regained."

"How?" she asked, sounding fragile.

In answer, I sank to kneeling in front of her. "This time I will not bite."

I STARTED SLOWLY, pushing her skirt up and pushing her knees wide. She fought me for a surprised second and then relented, her chest heaving as her breath came fast. She'd never known the kiss of a real man, one whose heat and magic could answer her own – and I was on that precipice again, torn between building her up or tearing her apart.

I decided to be gentle. A caged beast for a caged girl, yes.

I held her thighs apart and ran my tongue over the smooth petals of her pussy, pressing and sucking at the top where they joined, waiting for her lips to swell like an unfurling flower and open for me.

"Zaan –" she whispered my name and lay back, giving herself over. I pressed my tongue in deeply, and tasted the honey that a real woman should have.

I slid one hand up underneath her dress for her breast. She made a small moan and writhed as my fingers traced its curve and swirled closer to her nipple. I kept sucking at her, running my tongue over her most sensitive spot, and brought my other hand up, to press fingers into her.

She cried out at this, and her hips started to bob. I moved with them as they did, following her with my hand and my mouth, pinching her nipple gently. Her magic was in her now, I could feel the swirling power of it, recharging what she'd lost – and I pulled back.

"Zaan –" she breathed my name again, looking down at me with half-lidded eyes.

"Shhhh," I told her.

She gave me a questioning look, until I started licking her again.

I waited as her magic swelled and her entire body needed to be released. I felt her pussy pull at my fingers, trying to hold them in, as her highest petal rolled fat against my tongue, and her nipple was so taut that she gasped every time I brushed it – then I pulled back again.

"Zaan!" she begged sharply.

"You have your magic. This is mine."

She made a pained sound, and lay back.

I took her through three more rounds, times when her magic was crashing around me, clamoring for a release that only I could give. Wetness spilled from her against my chin and her breath came in a series of unending moans, and her hands sought purchase against the cushions she lay on or winding in my hair.

"Zaan – please – please –" she begged as the next round rose. "My King, please –" she said.

And something in the way she said it broke me. I growled and buried my face in her, sucking her hard, hand clawing around her breast, and shoving my fingers deep inside her pussy. She started shouting incoherently out, writhing under my mouth, hips flailing against the couch's soft cushions.

"My King, my King," she sobbed as her release wracked through her, and I felt the unchanneled swirl of her magic pass me by. We would have to find a way to harness it and aim it, until it became second nature to her. I tried to think of ways that we could do that, purposefully ignoring my painfully engorged cock until my erection subsided.

She lay panting on her couch and took her time pulling her hand out of my hair, before scooting backward as though she were afraid to touch me.

"Do you feel better?" I asked her, wiping my mouth with the back of one hand.

"I do."

"Good." I stood, in perfect control of myself again.

"Thank you for that," she said, pushing herself up on her elbows.

"You're welcome." I took a seat beside her and faced her as she pushed her skirts back down. "Now tell me what happens in five days."

He expected to have a normal conversation with me after that? For as much as he hated machines, he might as well have been one.

I pushed myself to sitting. I did feel better now. Stronger. And neither Joshan nor Beza had ever stirred such need inside me. They were skilled, but he was adept – I hadn't needed to give him a single command, he'd just known. He had read me like I was a book, and at the memories, I felt things flutter again inside.

"Tide's Day is five days away. The day when we were supposed to be married."

"I went to the traitor's domicile and overheard her talking with someone else. She had an image of you, on one of your screens."

"Really?"

"You were talking about helping people. They claimed it made you innocent."

Innocent I was. Not physically, maybe, but in all the other ways of the world.

"And she said that not even the high councilman could speed up the sun."

"So we have until then?"

"If they do not decide to kill you in the meantime." He looked around the chamber. "I wish you slept in a place with doors."

"But you said yourself the palace is airtight."

"Almost airtight, or I could not escape." He stood at this and began pacing. "The entire palace appears covered by a thick metal shell. They could bomb it – bombs are –"

"I know what bombs are, I've read of them," I said.

"But there are so many tunnels here there'd be no guarantee you were dead. And poisonous gases – the volume they would have to pump in to kill you would be astounding. I put nothing past them, though."

"You don't even know who *they* are."

"I will. I have to protect you."

"To save yourself." I watched him.

"Of course." He turned toward me with a malevolent grin. "I'm the last living Zaibann in existence. I'm even more precious than you are."

I snorted, and fell back onto cushions and stared up at the shadows my bed's posters cast on my ceiling. "But why would anyone want me dead? I've never hurt anyone."

"That you know of. Who knows what they've been doing with the power that they've stolen?" He swung an arm at the dream cradle. "Did your screens tell you anything?"

"It was another history. More in-fighting, more death. And then an odd segue into a children's tale about a group of rebels trying to rescue a precious gem."

One of his eyebrows rose.

"I know it sounds foolish, but he's trying to tell us something. And the story didn't have an ending. Every other screen he's brought me so far has." I didn't want to show him the pages I'd written. I'd continued in the tone of the final child's tale – I wasn't done yet, but I thought Zaan would find the work I had done puerile. "He wanted to see me when I was done with it. I was going to call for him, tomorrow."

"That is good. Then I can follow him."

"But you won't hurt him –" I protested.

"That depends entirely on him." The look Zaan gave me then was frightening. "Eat food now, and rest. Your lessons will begin in earnest tonight," he said, and left my chambers.

I WATCHED him go until he turned down the hall. Tomorrow was my one chance to prove Yzin trustworthy and all I had were a few hand-written pages to try to tell him that I knew I was the jewel – and I wanted to be saved already.

If I was wrong though, what would happen? Would I be springing some kind of trap? Would he shove me into the cradle and lock it until I never woke up again?

But that was too easy. If they'd wanted to do that, they could have done it any day prior.

I got up and paced, much as Zaan had. So what was the point of deceiving me every day, for three hundred years? Just to rob me of my powers?

Up until now, I'd never had a way to regain them so fast. I stopped and closed my eyes, remembering Zaan's mouth upon me, the things he'd done to me, the way he'd made me feel – I'd never felt such a build-up of power inside me before. I'd tried to tease myself, ordering Joshan to prolong things, but I had never been half as patient – or half as cruel. Where had he learned such things?

Airelle.

My ancestor who was in all ways better than me. Stronger, more beautiful, fiercer, so much more wise.

How many times had her hips risen beneath his tongue? And how many times had he mounted her to take his own release? I wanted him to push his cock inside me, I longed to feel my thighs slicked with his seed. But if he hadn't wanted me today, when I begged for him, when would he? Was my weakness the only thing that made him kind?

Would he ever see my strength?

Would I?

Beza appeared in the doorway with another tray of food. "My Queen," she said, offering them to me.

"Thank you, but no." He'd told me to rest, but I couldn't – I need to do something, to show myself and him – I set the tray down and laced my fingers through Beza's and pulled her down the hall.

10

To my trained warrior's eye, the palace was as easy to attack as it was difficult to defend. I paced through the halls, looking for natural bottlenecks where obstacles could be placed to slow intruders down. There were some, but not enough.

And what did I have to block them with? Couches, ancient art? I grimly imagined an army slashing through a flower display.

That wasn't even counting the machines. When I'd been entombed, Rix knowledge was fearsome enough. It'd advanced impossibly in the meantime.

What would happen if I couldn't channel Ilylle's power in any meaningful way?

Or what if I could, and they walked in with weapons that were modified cradles, draining her and pulling me apart?

The alternative though was to give up. I'd already seemingly died once – I had no intention of coming so close to it again.

I started searching for the tools I'd need to teach her.

WHEN BEZA WAS DONE DRESSING me and braiding up my hair, I admired myself in my mirror. The clothes I wore were variations on what I'd read, long dresses made from dark heavy fabrics, and my hair was adapted from ancient portraits that we'd both seen, piled high and pinned with sticks that ended in diamond stars. Last, but not least, the collar was directly from Zaan's mouth. Its thick black leather fit me snugly from chin to chest.

I looked powerful. Exactly like Queens in the ancient portraits did. Perhaps looking like Airelle was half the battle of becoming her? I prayed that it would be.

I walked back to my chambers and sat down in front of my desk where my story waited for me. I would have to figure out an ending before tomorrow.

"My Queen," said a voice behind me, and I turned. Zaan stood in the hallway, holding a bag. His dark eyes flashed over me until his gaze settled on my collared neck. "Are you denying me blood, now?"

"No. I just hoped this would make you more comfortable." I plucked at one long burgundy sleeve.

"What care you for my comfort?"

"You are my King."

"In name alone. I was wed to Airelle, and that cannot be undone."

I closed my eyes. Clearly, my plan had been foolish – "I do not seek to undo it –"

"Do you want to learn or not?" he said, stepping past me. "Or is your life just a game?"

I sat straighter. "I do want to learn. I have to, for myself and for my people."

"Good." He pulled out an object I didn't recognize out of his bag and placed it on the desk. "I found this deep inside the palace. Let us begin." He formally held his hand out to me. I took it and let him pull me to standing.

. . .

WE WALKED side by side for a moment and I felt like a Queen of old as he gestured me to the bed. I sat down on it primly, the tree-like posters arcing high overhead, listening as he spoke.

"That," he said, pointing to the thing he'd left behind, "is a candle. It's meant to burn. They provided light, before those –" he waved a hand at the lights overhead, and went on. "You've never been forced to refine your powers, they come out of you in an unruly wave. You need to learn to control them, to pinpoint where they go, and what they do."

I felt my eyebrows creep up my forehead. "You want me to create flame?"

"I do."

"But...how?"

His lips quirked up in a cruel smile. "I will show you. But first, take off that silly dress."

The dress was hard to take off without Beza, the fastens were high and tight, but I managed to reach them without ruining my hair and I chose not to take off the collar. The dress fell to the ground in a rush, leaving me standing naked inside its circle.

He stepped up to me, still carrying his bag, and reached out, running his hand behind my neck and up into my hair, his fingers tangling into my braids, bringing me into the circle of his arms for a kiss.

As his lips met mine, mine parted and let his tongue in. He leaned forward with the force of his kiss, his body pressing against mine, as his tongue owned my mouth – there was no other word. I fought against the onslaught of his intent and then released, softening beneath him, letting him hold and control me, from his kiss on downward.

I had never felt wanted so deeply before – too bad it was all a lie to teach me lessons.

When he pulled back a minute later I felt light, and he stayed so close that all I could see was him.

"Ready for your teaching?" he asked softly, rumbling the words. I nodded, helpless.

"Good." He stepped back and overturned his bag. A spool of rope came tumbling out. He took up one end of this, and fastened it to my wrist. "Turn around," he commanded. I did so, and then watched with innocent amazement as he tied the other end to one of the posters of my bed.

He did the same thing on the other side, cutting off the extra rope with a serving knife. I fought against the ties lightly and found I couldn't get free. "What are you doing?"

"Preparing to teach you," he said – and landed the first blow. I heard a whistle through the air and then felt a stinging thud on my ass.

"Ow!" I leapt forward, trapped by my tethered arms. "What was that –" I twisted, looking over my shoulder to see. He held something – it looked like a whip, like a lot of whips at once.

"I spent today being busy," he said, stroking where he'd just hit. "Your palace didn't have what I needed, so I made accommodations."

"But – why are you hitting me?"

I heard him take a step back. "To teach you to focus," he said, with a smack. "To teach you to listen," he said with another one. "To teach you control," he said, and hit me with a third.

I yelped and gasped with each blow's landing. "But –"

"Be quiet," he said, hitting me again. "Is the pain intolerable? Be honest."

I was breathing faster. I'd never been trapped before – in my own palace, no less – and they did hurt, but...I could take more. "No."

"Good. Let me know if it becomes so. Until then, though," he said, landing the next blow atop a shoulder blade.

Each blow landing burned and stung with a sudden wave of pain that disappeared as quickly as it'd come. I had to separate the surprise of being hit with the actual pain of the blow – once I began to expect blows, getting hit was easier, if still frustrating.

"How is this supposed to –"

He smacked across my ass again and I rose on my toes with a shout. My eyes stung, watering, and I hovered, as if trying to get away from him.

"You were saying?" he asked, stepping forward to run his hand over me. My whole body trembled at his touch, frightened there might be more – and perversely frightened that there might not.

"That hurt," I said, when I could breathe.

"I know." Zaan's hand traced the contours of my ass again. "It is supposed to."

He stepped back and then blows rained down on me, one after another after another. Across my back, down my back, across my ass, across my thighs – I didn't know what to expect, only that I needed to expect, that there was no escape from what was surely this madman behind me. I cried out and shuddered, twisting this way and that, rising high up on my toes, my whole body looking for a way out involuntarily.

Then the blows stopped and he leaned forward to growl in my ear. "Stop moving."

"Why?"

"Because you need to learn to ride the pain. Right now, the pain is riding you." He snapped whatever he held behind me and I jumped. He snorted in disgust. "How can you be the Queen of a people if you cannot rule yourself?"

"I am a Queen," I said through gritted teeth. He reached underneath one arm to cup my left breast in his palm. I trembled at his touch, and then slowly sank back down into my heels, relaxing my body though my entire back and ass stung.

A second of comfort later, and his thumb and forefinger found my nipple and began to pinch it, hard. I didn't realize how hard – compared to the rest of my body, it didn't hurt – and then it did, oh how it did, it was like being burned. I grit my teeth harder and my hands clenched into fists, but I didn't cry out or move.

When he released me, I sagged forward, making a silent scream as blood rushed back in and different nerves sung.

When I could breathe again, I stood straight. It had hurt, yes, but I'd survived. Me, who lived in this palace full of gilt and cushions, who wasn't accustomed to pain. I swallowed and looked over my shoulder at him in pride.

"I will not give you the satisfaction of breaking me."

Zaan stepped forward, his entire body pressed against mine, making all the parts of it he'd whipped sting – he rubbed against me on purpose, and I could feel the jutting stiffness of his cock.

"Don't worry about me, my Queen. I will be taking my satisfaction in other ways."

Then he stepped back, and the blows began again.

IT WAS as it had been when I was on the couch before him, with his mouth on the darkness between my thighs. Whereas then he'd made me ride waves of pleasure, now he made me ride waves of pain, seeing how much I could take, pushing me again and again almost to my breaking point.

My pride stopped me from crying out again – but my pride couldn't keep me still, as my body wisely tried to escape, and Zaan stopped.

"Do you hate me?" he asked.

I sunk down, hanging from my arms, feeling all my blood rush inside. "I do."

"Good. Hate and power live side-by-side. Burn the candle."

"I can't."

"You can. You just don't want to, badly enough." He hit me with the ropes again, and this time I cried out.

"I can't even see the candle!" I only knew it was behind me.

"All the better. When you manage it, I will be more impressed."

"But – my powers –" I protested.

"They're still inside you." He took a step forward and put the palm of his hand on my ass. I flinched and then relaxed as he stroked it down, his fingers in my cleft until his hand slipped between my thighs. "Focus, Ilylle –" he said, pushing a finger into me. I made a small noise, and tilted my hips back so that he could have more – and his free hand smacked my ass. I yelped and rocked forward, but his hand moved with me, and his body again pressed behind mine, catching me on purpose, scraping his buckles against my welted skin, his free hand pinching my breast, armpits, and stomach, hard, whispering, "Focus, Ilylle – focus –" as his other hand pulsed in and out of my dark place.

My power was on me in a rush, a thick cloud of it, choking the air around me. Zaan made a primal noise at this, and I could feel his erection rub against my thigh. "Focus, Ilylle. The power is yours – it's always been yours. Take it inside of you and then set it free."

I twisted my head and body, trying to get away from his attention or fall into it in turns, riding up and down on his hand, feeling the rubbing of his cock against my leg. I stayed in that moment, on that brink between decision and abandonment and saw the candle in my mind, and called for it to spark as I went off. I shouted, as he pinched, as his hand pressed, as a cold buckle pressed hot skin, and then I roiled as I felt my power consume me. I was the flame I called out, and every piece of me burned.

I went limp after that. Zaan caught me, holding me up long enough to free my hands, and then carefully lay me down atop my bed. I couldn't move, my arms were sore, my back – there was no part of it that didn't sting – my calves were cramping and my breasts felt swollen. But despite all that pain, I didn't feel like I was a part of my body anymore. I'd lifted away from it, moved beyond it. I was finally free from the palace, and from myself. I was spinning.

"Look," Zaan said, taking my chin and moving my head. I didn't believe what I saw, not until I blinked my eyes.

The candle was burning. One tiny flame. I'd done that – my magic had done that. I could be like Airelle – Zaan was right – *I* was right. I was a Queen.

Then a zoomer crawled into the chamber, jumped up onto the desk, and reached out with a paw to put the candle out.

I LAY BESIDE ILYLLE, watching her breathe. Now that she knew what she was capable of – I wouldn't have to take her that far the next time.

Had I ever pushed Airelle that hard?

I didn't think I had.

I'd always been bound by love for her. What great heights could we have reached if instead we were bound by blood and hate? Too late to wonder, now.

Ilylle's whole back was a map of red. I knew how fast she healed – my blood-kiss upon her thigh was gone. But even though she wouldn't see what I had wrought upon her in a day, it'd still be in her mind. She would never forget what I had done to her. For her.

Nor I forget what she had done to me. I'd come alongside her, her magic draining my cock, making my seed wet and stain the fabric by my thigh.

I had always been a man of precision and control – that was what it meant to be a Zaibann. Without it, I would have blown away the first time I ever transformed – or been one of the Zaibann who chose not to transform, castrated by fear, never attempting to use their own powers.

I hadn't wanted release – I'd envisioned conquering her fully, then untying her and pulling her head down to fuck her face with my cock. But the call of her magic had caught me unprepared and I'd released with a shout the same as she had, unable to stop myself.

At the thought of her raw power dredging through me, my cock stirred, just as Ilylle twisted her head to drowsily look up.

"Is our lesson done?"

Beastly need flowed through me for a second time. "No," I said, reaching for her neck.

I spread my legs, pushing apart the fabric that hid my cock from her. "Come here, girl," I commanded, pushing her head down to my hips. Her body sank willingly under my control, and a second later her lips were wrapped around my shaft.

"Yes," I groaned, a guttural sound. I took a handful of her hair so that it pulled against her scalp and moved her up and down. She'd taken control away from me minutes ago – now I wanted to take control away from her. Her lips tightened on my shaft and pulled as I raised her, holding her high to suck the head of me, before I shoved her back down, making her gag on my cock, feeling myself bob at the back of her throat.

For her part, she didn't fight, she let me make her ride me, taking what I gave her as my hips thrust up and my fist in her hair shoved her down. She made small noises, of weakness, of submission, but I didn't relent because her lips and tongue wouldn't stop sucking, even when I'd almost pulled her off of me, her tongue pressed against the bottom of my cock, licking against my head, searching out the spot that opened into me – I ran both hands into her hair and made her take all of me, holding her to me as my ass tightened, pushing more of me into her, her spit too much for her mouth, dripping down my balls – I took her like that, three times, head to hilt, hilt to head, and then came hard, spilling the second course of my seed inside her mouth. I spasmed bodily, and kept thrusting, again and again, until my cock started going soft and I released her, hairpins falling out of her tangled braids.

Ilylle looked up at me, her lips red and swollen. "My King," she whispered, her blue-eyes misted with some emotion, I knew not what.

She'd swallowed my seed. She'd swallowed every drop.

"My Queen," I acknowledged her, and then let my head fall back onto her bed.

11

We lay there together, silent. Time passed. Her unreal servants brought in a tray of food. I, however, needed other nourishment.

I sat up, covering myself again, looking down at her welted naked skin. "Are you all right?"

She looked up and gave me a nervous smile. "Are you?"

"I am."

She tucked her head back down, bringing one hand to her chin. From her position on the bed, she could see the desk and candle. "It worked, didn't it."

"It did."

"What now? Or dare I ask?"

"More lessons – later." I moved to stand beside the bed. "I need to go back out to check on the councilman's plans – and I need your blood."

Ilylle nodded, without raising her head. Instead she offered me a hand.

I took it like I was pulling her to dance, then swung it wide. Hands and wrists were no good if one was concerned with making marks, no matter how temporary. I bowed, like a horse drinking from a fountain, and carefully bit into her inner upper arm.

She cried out softly as my teeth sank through her flesh. At least this time if she fainted, she'd already be lying down. I sucked at the wounds I'd made, working at her with my teeth and tongue, until enough blood flowed that I was sated. This time, I carefully cleaned my mess, licking the last drop up from her and off my lips before rising.

"Thank you," I said, standing again.

"You're welcome," she said, folding her arm back in.

"I'll be back soon. Do not get into your cradle," I told her, and she nodded. I walked off down the hall towards the metal-way-out and had a feeling I'd find her in that same spot when I returned.

I WATCHED Zaan leave until I couldn't see him anymore or hear his steps.

Zaan had given me his seed. I ran my tongue around the inside of my mouth, wondering at the salty earthy taste of him, so different from Joshan. He wanted me. Not just keeping me alive and teaching me my powers for his own sake, no, that last part had been all him, him needing me to suck him.

I had never felt so wanted before, and fresh power stirred, not in my hips but in my chest. I was wanted by my Zaibann – he'd needed me so badly that he couldn't resist. I trailed a hand over my welts and bruises, hips and breasts, and finally felt strong.

Joshan entered the room, coming in to retrieve the tray. "My Queen," he said, noticing my eyes upon him.

I rolled over on my side to face him. "Am I beautiful, Joshan?"

"Of course, my Queen."

He would service me and he would feign enjoyment of it, but he didn't have needs like Zaan – Joshan would never bow my head to make me take him in my mouth.

But my slave did still have his uses. I got up and went to the desk, picking up the candle. "Are there others of these in the palace?"

Joshan looked at it and then nodded. "Yes, my Queen."

"Bring them to me. Bring me all of them."

"My Queen," he agreed, and bowed before walking out.

That finished, I picked up the dress that had fallen and carried it over to my chair, to cushion my sore bottom while I wrote.

I THREW AWAY the last three pages I'd written for Yzin – honestly, I spent half an hour trying to call up enough power to burn them, I was so shamed by what I'd written. The ending of the story had been about the jewel waiting to be rescued, hoping that someday the rebels would find her, if only they got to her in time.

I crumpled them and threw them to the floor so zoomers would carry them off and started fresh.

No, instead the ending of this final story would be about how the girl trapped inside the jewel broke free – then burned the palace down around her.

JOSHAN RETURNED HOURS LATER, just as my story was almost complete, dragging a large box. "I believe these were what you wanted, my Queen," he said, opening it.

It was full of candles of all shapes and sizes. "Excellent work, Joshan."

I swept my papers aside and lined up the candles front to back and side to side, all facing the bed. "Is there anything else, my Queen?" Joshan asked when we were through.

"Yes," I said, prying up a bent wick with a fingernail. "Go to my bed. I'll meet you there in a second."

When I was done arranging the candles in perfect height order, my entire desk covered in sweet smelling wax, I turned and saw Joshan standing where I'd told him to, patiently.

"Oh, Joshan," I said, shaking my head at him.

"Yes, my Queen?" he asked, eager to please. He cared for me, in his own machine way, but now that I had Zaan I knew I needed so much more.

Still, though – I crawled up onto my bed and walked over to him on my knees to take his hand. "Come," I said, and pulled him on the bed beside me. Then I took his shoulders and pushed him down, head up but facing the end of the bed. As I was still naked it was an easy thing to straddle his chest.

The only part of me that didn't hurt from Zaan's lesson was my pussy – which was good because it was the only part I needed to make this experiment work.

I rose up and crawled forward, till my knees were by his neck, my dark place inches from his mouth. "I need you to taste me, Joshan. You know how I like it."

"I do, my Queen," he answered, and then I lowered myself down.

His lips lapped at me as I sank slowly, his tongue tracing the outside of my folds, and up underneath my hood, before my petals parted to let him in.

After that, everything was simple – his tongue thrust up into me, where Zaan's fingers had just been – and then licked forward, sucking my most sensitive spot.

For my part, I crouched over him on all fours, knees spread wide. My magic was already alive, I could feel it surging, up and down my spine and thighs. I held myself up on one arm and cradled my other breast, pulling that nipple tight – and then looked at the candles. They would burn. I wanted them to burn. I would call down fire upon them, and all of them would light.

Joshan's tongue didn't stop and neither did I – any time I felt too close I clawed myself back to attention.

The power was mine. It was in me. I controlled it. All of it.

The nearest candle flickered and hissed. Seeing it light mesmerized me, and I sank, grinding more of my pussy into Joshan's face, his chin pressing in as his mouth sucked and tongue lapped.

The next candle, and the next one, the one after that – all of them took, one row, two rows, four, twelve – until every candle on my desk was waving a tiny spot of flame – just like the tiny spot between my legs that Joshan licked.

"Joshan!" I shouted as I came, bobbing my hips down deeper into him, clawing my hands into my bedding as I released. "Joshan –"

Zoomers – ten of them – crawled into the room and up the desk and made short work of quenching all the candles.

"I did it –" I said, propping myself back up. "Did you see that?" I asked him.

"See what, my Queen?" he asked, looking only up.

I laughed. It didn't matter. I knew what I'd done. I lay down and rolled over and saw Beza in the doorway, waiting.

"Did you see that, Beza?"

She shook her head. "No, my Queen."

I looked between them. "Neither of you? You're no fun."

Beza took several steps over to the bed. "We do like to play with you, my Queen."

I smiled softly and flung my arms out – and found Joshan's hard cock pressing against my palm. I slipped my hand between the folds of his robe and took hold of him because it pleased me to do so, just as my mouth had pleased Zaan, and I traced his outline with a fingertip.

Why? Who would make a machine this thoroughly? And towards what end? Why would anyone care if I knew how to take a man?

Did someone know that fucking would unlock my magic from inside of me? If so, how?

"Joshan, sit up." My hand went with him as he moved, until he was kneeling on my bed, looking back at me. "Beza – come here."

"My Queen," she said, and let me pull her onto the bed. I wrapped my hands into her hair as Zaan had trapped mine, and pushed her mouth down to take Joshan's cock. He groaned as she throated him, and like a jacar's kitten she began to purr.

I watched her take him, rocking back and forth, arms and ass as he stood still, hips thrust slightly forward. I pushed her hair back so I could see how far her lips slid up his shaft, and how wet his cock was when it slid back out.

"Keep going," I commanded, getting another idea. I ran to my desk and found a candle roughly the size and shape of a cock, and returned to my bed. I flipped up Beza's hem, until her perfectly curved ass swayed in front of me with each of her mouth's strokes. I stroked both soft sides of her ass and then reached between them and down to find her dark place with one finger – and then gently pushed the candle in.

Beza moaned, muffled by Joshan's cock in her throat.

"Is that good?" I asked her, stroking her back. She made another pleasured muffled sound, and rocked back farther toward my hand.

"Good," I whispered back. My magic stirred in me again as I orchestrated them – whatever Zaan had done had broken walls and now I felt it rushing, trapped inside me, like a lilan fluttering against a gilded cage – it needed a way out.

I pressed the candle in another inch. Then two, watching her petals push open as if grasping to take more of the candle inside. I reached around her to touch her bright spot, circling it before rubbing it carefully, while pulsing the candle in and out.

"Can you take this, my Beza? Can you take so much more?" I felt the thrill of the conqueror controlling her, just as Zaan had done to me. At the head of the bed, Joshan's hands were tangled in her hair.

I started fucking her with the candle, using it just like a cock. She moaned, the sound still muffled, but her honey spilled out over my fingers, and I was tempted to pull away to taste a drop – but no – I rubbed the top of her folds so gently, and then became more rough, feeling her body rock with the thrusts of the candle, her mouth trapped around Joshan's cock.

Everything about her was still for a moment, and I knew she was on the verge of release. I pounded the candle into her as my fingers sped up and in moments she was screaming against Joshan.

Good Joshan, loyal Joshan, had waited until that moment – but now his hips thrust madly against her face, pulling on her hair the same way Zaan had mine, until he made a guttural sound, and pulled back.

"My Queen," he said, a look of worry in his eye.

"Good, Joshan –"

"No – my Queen –" he untangled a hand from Beza's hair and pointed behind me.

I turned, and gasped.

EMPOWERED BY ILYLLE'S BLOOD, I surged down the halls in my smoke form, finding the exit and wending my way out and down, until my feet landed on the road outside, unseen.

The marker I'd left on the woman called to me. It was closer this time though, so I followed it as a man, changing my smoke-armor to match what other men wore on the street.

Daylight did not do the city around the palace any favors. Refuse piled on corners where children ferretted through it with small hands. I didn't know what they were looking for – I didn't want to know. This was so different from Aranda of my time. There'd been poverty, yes, but the very air stank of desperation here – desperation and the foul breaths the metal beasts put out as they traveled on the roads. I had to leap out of their way several times, the drivers inside not seeing or caring if they hit me.

Soon my marker led me to a sewer grate inside a long alley. I looked down at it and frowned. I could turn into smoke to get in, but I didn't know what was below, and as smoke I could be trapped. I waited, hoping the woman with the marker would emerge, but when she didn't I dissipated myself and sunk in.

I stayed near the ceiling of the sewer, following her pull. There were just as many tunnels under here as there had been in the palace – in fact, if my sense of place was accurate, I had doubled back beneath the ground to be near the palace's underbelly.

Why was that woman down here? I knew I was getting close, the pull was stronger – I reached what I knew would be a final door, and sunk below it, finding the woman and several others in a heated conversation.

"We've got to do it now, Elissa."

The men she conversed with were wearing strange armor, covered in metals, and they stood to one side of a massive Rixan beast. It was the size of one of the metal-beasts outside roaming the roads, but it had a proboscis of sharp spinning wheels that narrowed down to point. I had never seen its like before, but I could use my imagination – it was the worm I'd heard her speak of, and they meant to breech the Feather Palace's lower walls.

"The historian says he needs another day."

The leader of the armored men put his hand on the hilt of some weapon. I recognized the gesture from my own past – and the note of exasperation in his voice. "What difference will a day make?"

"You saw the tape – she doesn't know about the outside world – about any of it. She can still be converted to our side. He goes to speak to her again."

"And hopes she finally gets his gist? She's been dense for three-hundred years now – that's ten times as long as I've been alive." Other men grunted at this.

"How about we go and talk to her ourselves?" said one of them, patting the side of the metal-monster they stood beside.

Elissa's eyes narrowed and she looked among them coolly. "Remember that this plan is his plan – and that without him, we would not have this chance."

"And you're sure he hasn't changed his mind? I mean, he waits long enough and he gets to live forever."

"It has taken him a thousand years to infiltrate up until this point. So yes, he plays a longer game than you and I can comprehend – but he is not a liar." She looked among them, waiting for one of them to challenge her. "You'll have your answer today. But make no move till then."

The man nearest her ground his jaw but then shrugged. "If he's truly waited a thousand years, I can wait twenty-four more hours. After that, though –"

"Understood." Elissa nodded curtly and left the room. I swirled up to where the metal-beast was aimed, and marked the wall.

. . .

It took me time to flow out and double-back to the palace again, but Ilylle's blood kept me strong until I reformed and started walking down the halls.

How had she lived for three hundred years? And Yzin for a thousand? The magically inclined lived longer, healthier, but one lifetime was enough for any man.

A clicking sound echoed through the halls. Had the men outside decided to release their machine? I ran forward to where my hall joined a larger one and saw a herd of zoomers racing eight-leggedly toward Ilylle's great chamber and instantly changed to smoke to follow them.

I reached her room as they did – half of it was on fire and she was madly laughing, starting new flames just as quickly as zoomers could put them out. I gathered myself and swirled around the room's perimeter, extinguishing all the flames out in my passage before reforming in front of her. She was naked, standing beside her bed where her two servants lay.

"Are you mad?"

Ilylle looked suitably chastened. "No. It's just – I can do it now. I just wanted to see –" she pointed at her couch, and a flame arose from the center cushion. The nearest zoomer sprung atop it and extinguished it, then switched paws. Needle and thread emerged, and it began to patch the hole. "See?"

"I see."

She crossed her room and pulled on a robe, tying its sash loosely. "All I had to do was help Joshan fuck Beza and –" she made a gesture, indicating the surrounding destruction – the marks on the ceiling, the ruined tapestries, the pile of melted wax. And as if to defy me, she grinned, and lit a different spot on the couch alight.

I'd left her unsated? When I thought she could take no more? I would not be making that mistake again. I slashed my hand through the air. "All this is impressive, but you need to stop."

"But I have power now!" she said, leaning forward. Her robe slipped open, showing the belly-curve of one round breast. I thought of throwing her on the bed and fucking her until we set the room ablaze, but I didn't let it show.

"Power, without control, is nothing." I stepped back from her and surveyed the room's destruction. "Right now you're as likely to immolate your people as you are to save them." When my gaze returned to her I saw her shoulders fall. "Though I am glad you have learned how to access it on your own. It seems we will not need to fuck again."

I watched her when I said it. I wanted to see the effect it would have on her – if what I gave her could be so easily replaced with metal-puppets. The look she gave me then was dark and pained, and something low inside me stirred. I knew then I'd planted a hook inside her, but she answered, "Whatever you think best, my King."

"Precisely," I said. The first wave of zoomers started leaving the room, now that they'd caught up with her destruction. I sat down on the couch, inspecting the hole that'd just been fixed, unable to tell a flame had ever been there.

12

"Tell me more about Yzin," he commanded, from his spot on the couch. I tugged my robe closed and tied it tighter so that none of my skin showed. He didn't want to fuck me anymore? Why? Had I done something wrong? I walked back to my bed and sat on it, half a room away from him.

"He's always been a councilmember. He's the one that taught me how to read – and then gave me the screens, as I've told you."

"And he's been with you for all three hundred of your years?"

I nodded.

"Has he aged?"

I licked my lips in thought. Time passed so slowly for me – but in memories of Yzin from when I was younger, he was too. "A little, yes. His joints creak now."

My King's eyes narrowed and he nodded. "When is he coming?"

Joshan answered for me. "In an hour, my Queen."

Oh no. If Joshan had told me that, I wouldn't have laid waste to my room. An hour wasn't much time. "Beza –" I needed to be bathed, my hair needed tending, and I needed a new dress.

At least my story was done. I'd been sure to put it in my desk's bottom drawer, safe from flame.

Zaan stood and crossed the room, picking something up off of the floor. The collar that I'd worn when he'd seen me last. He ran its leather through his fingers and then looked to me.

"Do you think we can trust him?"

I laughed once, harshly. "What do I know of trust?"

His gaze was critical. "You may trust in me."

"Only because you don't want to die." I leaned down and picked up the dress I'd worn the night before and snatched the collar from his hand.

"Indulge my curiosity and wear it," he said, jerking his chin at the collar.

"As my King desires," I said, and walked out.

I TRIED to find solace in the waters of my pool, or in the sensation of Beza coming my long hair out, in the pulling on of dresses and taking them off again until I wore one that was just right – all the small things that used to satisfy me every day and night before he had come along.

Before I had released *him*.

Part of me wished I had never found that book, or figured out how it might be read. Then I would never know the depths of my betrayal, or feel half as useless as I did now. Zaan was right, catching things on fire wouldn't feed Mazaria. Airelle had been built for war – but there were no wars anymore as far as Yzin's screens told me, just vast inequalities between people who had everything and people who had nothing. I needed to figure out how to be built for peace.

When I returned to my great chambers, the zoomers were done cleaning and it looked none the worse for my morning's exercise.

I walked over to my desk and pulled open the bottom drawer – and the pages I'd hidden inside were gone. Some overzealous zoomer had claimed them.

"No!" I said, bunching my hands into fists.

"No, what? Is something troubling you, my dear?"

I turned and found Yzin there, standing calmly in the doorway, his eyebrows high.

"No – everything's fine," I said and gave him a smile. I hoped that it would be. Without the pages, I would have to tell him my ending myself.

I walked across the room to my couch and sat down, gesturing for him to join me. He did so, slowly, and pushed extra pillows behind himself to prop himself up.

And when he was arranged, he turned to look at me. I couldn't help but notice the way his eyes flickered to my collar. "Do you like it?" I asked, hoping I would be able to read something into his response.

His gaze traced my face, trying to read me as much as I was him. "I do," he said at last. "Did you enjoy the screen?"

"Up until the ending. It just stopped. But you knew that."

He nodded sagely. "Not all stories have endings yet."

"Well I think this one should," I said. I crossed my hands in my lap to gather strength before speaking again. "I didn't like the way that it was going, and so I wrote my own ending. Why shouldn't the woman trapped in the jewel help to get herself out? Does everyone think she's just happy inside there, with only gemstone for company?"

Yzin's expression lifted and he leaned forward. "It's easy to assume things from the outside when gemstone is all you see."

"In my story, she learns how to fight and she practices, and when the rebels come for her she's ready to go with them, and they all make their escape, tearing down the palace behind them."

He went still before responding. "Do you mean what you say, my Queen? Or is it just a story to you?"

Was this a final test of loyalty, or was Yzin really on my side? It didn't matter. The truth needed to be free.

"I mean every word I say. I always have."

He crumpled in front of me. "I have waited so long for this day – and it is almost too late." His hands reached for mine and clasped them tight. "Do you know what you are – do you understand what I've been trying to tell you of the world outside?"

I nodded. "I do, finally."

Zaan reformed behind him. He had a weapon with him, a sword, and I didn't know where in the palace he'd found it, but he was pointing it at Yzin.

"Traitor, turn around."

Yzin sat straighter at the sound of Zaan's voice and did as he was told. "Can it be?" He turned, and laughed. "Zaan!" Yzin named him, as if he were an old friend. Zaan's eyes narrowed, then widened.

"Rkatrayzin. I did not recognize you. You do not smell as you once did."

"You – know each other?" I blinked between them.

Zaan placed the tip of his weapon at the side of Yzin's neck, just below his ear. "We do. Tell me how she died. Now."

Yzin looked from him to me and back again. "She didn't."

"What do you mean she didn't die? This one tells me it's been twenty-thousand years –"

"It has been." Yzin let go of my hands to push the blade away from himself.

"How have you lived that long? And if Airelle is alive, where is she?"

"I will answer, I will answer," Yzin said, waving his hands. Zaan stepped back but stayed ready as Yzin looked to me. "In the vase – did you find and read the history?"

"I did."

Yzin sighed aloud. "Bless you for your learning, girl, and your unnatural curiosity."

"I'm threatening you, old man," Zaan growled.

"And if I were not prepared to die, I would not be here." Yzin said, waving Zaan nearer to me. "Move over so that I may see you both. I am, as you said, an elder."

Zaan said something uncouth in his old tongue, but stepped sideways so that Yzin could look at both of us easily. Yzin's eyes lingered on Zaan, almost hungrily. "I never thought the day would come when I would again see a Zaibann walking among us again."

"But the other Kings?" I asked.

"Oh, my Queen, how many lies you've been told," Yzin said with a head-shake. "But that ends now, I swear it."

"You'll have to pardon my disbelief," Zaan said.

"You have every right to be angry, Zaibann. I knew Airelle, and I know who you were to her. I was there." Yzin looked over to me. "I had a small rank in the old court. A ceremonial one – historian. Most who held that title ignored it, but not me. I knew great things were happening, and I wanted the world to know ages later, when it would forget."

Yzin pushed himself further back in the cushions. "I traveled with the army and got into the council. Airelle was fond of me – or of having someone write her exploits, at least. And so I was there when the decision was made to sacrifice her Zaibann for Aranda."

"Did you start plotting to betray her at that moment, then?" Zaan asked coldly. "Or did you wait an hour?"

Yzin ignored him, looking only at me. "You read the book but you weren't there. Times were dire. Our society was largely magic based, but only few possessed the power – and magic couldn't shield us from Rixan bombs. Shielding our borders via magic was our only chance – but what we wrought that day – you know most people do not live as long as Queens do, don't you?"

"I do. I read it on your screens."

"Those of us who were present that day, as Airelle siphoned off all the magic from her Zaibann, when Aranda closed its doors – we noticed things. We were more powerful. We healed more quickly. We were physically strong. Anyone possessed of powers who was present wound up changed."

He looked at Zaan. "We used the time you bought us to infiltrate the Rix, to bring back treasures. Our learned men undid their work and puzzled out their science. Within a year, safe in Aranda's bosom, we were close to catching up."

"But –" Zaan prompted, sword still out.

"But – by then the other councilmen were used to their new lives. Who didn't want more power, more strength? To undo what Airelle had done would undo those gifts as well. And so Railan led a coup against her."

"Airelle would have rather died than be captured."

"We did not give her a choice."

"You admit you were among their number?" Zaan's voice was low and tight.

"Railan murdered anyone who disagreed with him. I did not fight him – nor did I aide him – I merely watched in the name of history."

Zaan made a growling sound and I worried he might slice Yzin's head off before he finished his story.

"You see, Railan learned how to merge Rix technology and magic and created a device that could drain the power from a Queen and give it to others. He trapped Airelle in one and left her there."

"But you said she was still alive." Zaan pronounced every word as a threat.

"She is – in a manner of speaking," he said, and gestured broadly at me. My heart leapt into my throat as Yzin went on. "The people were too used to being led. So we took a piece of her, and cultivated a new Queen."

"Cultivated?" I whispered.

"Yes," he said, with a heavy nod. "Our first few experiments were tragic. Too much power, not enough sense – no sense at all, forms that just lay there, bereft of anything but basest life – or beings of so much power that they immolated themselves the second they hit puberty – Airelle was alive through all of these. We trotted her weakened form out at every celebration for our country, practically tied her to a pole and made her perform her duties, before tucking her back inside her box."

And I knew exactly what her box was – a variation on my dream cradle. My eyes flickered to the monstrosity. I would never let anyone put me in it again. It was hard not to look at it now, sitting by my bed, without setting it aflame.

"Eventually we got the knack of it and created a girl-child. One who we could mold. The process only took a thousand years. After that, lowering our borders and conquering the majority of the world was a mere formality."

The horrified expression on Zaan's face was mirrored on my own. Only Yzin seemed untroubled – he was just reporting history.

"It didn't do to give the girl too many powers – then she could kill a councilman. If the girls grew too willful, if they wanted to conquer things, or travel Aranda to see the land for themselves, we either drained these for our own benefit, or killed them if they proved too strong." Yzin shrugged, as though what he was telling us was commonplace. "Eventually, we settled on this arrangement. If we kept the girls in seclusion, not knowing anything of the outside world except the small bits that we showed them, emphasizing their weakness and our strength, it worked. We gave them mechanical servants to interact with to abate their loneliness, and we taught them enough to keep their minds occupied. They would live a few hundred years quietly, and when they got too strong and too restless, we would tell them about their King."

I felt my jaw drop, and looked to Zaan. The blade he held was shaking in anger.

"When a Queen dies, a flash of immense power is released. It is possible to trap this power, and use it to regenerate yourself, if you know how. But if you're too close to the Queen – say, you're the one that kills her – you'll be immolated. Several original councilmen died when they got too greedy and killed Queens out of hand." Yzin paused dramatically here, like he was giving me a childhood lesson he would quiz me on later. "But an angry Zaibann has no fear of death – so all we had to do was tell the girls the right story. They were so eager for something different in their lives – something new – that they all instantly believed."

Just like I had. Yzin was looking at me, his face somber. I nodded. "Go on."

"So we created a ceremony. One by one, we plucked Zaibanns up, used enough magic to give their stone cocks strut, and then gave them to the Queens as presents. Talk up the ceremony enough, the magic of their future lives, and they hardly mind being chained to a table and presented to their 'King'." Yzin said the word as ironically as possible. "Their mechanical servants push the table forward until they join, and her magic brings him back to life – her very own blood-starved mythological creature. The Zaibann kills the Queen, the Queen's death kills the Zaibann, empowering the councilmen for another few hundred years, and there you are."

13

There *I* was.

"I cannot believe that," Zaan said.

He couldn't, but I could. My life was even worse than I'd imagined.

"Is Airelle still alive?" Zaan moved the tip of his sword to emphasize each point.

"Depends on your definition of life, Zaibann. By some definitions, no – by some definitions, she's sitting right here beside me."

Zaan looked to me, his face clouded with confusion. "I don't understand –"

"Railan is the one in charge of creating clones. It's possible that he has her in a vat somewhere, or just a piece of her pinkie finger." Yzin shrugged.

"Are you saying I am Airelle?" My voice rose as I spoke. "If I am, then I should kill you for all you have done!"

Yzin put up a calming hand. "Ilylle, I have spent your lifetime watching over you. Teaching you – training you. You are the first Queen that I thought could make it outside the palace walls. You have no idea the lengths I've gone to help you prepare."

I crossed my arms to hold myself – I really was a copy of her – the final lie was that I wasn't even me. I turned toward Yzin, still reeling in horror. "All you did was put a book in a vase."

"That I then made sure your servants would take you to. It has taken me three thousand years to have enough spies in the palace network to make sure that their commands are mine alone. A normal man lives only eighty, and only works sixty of that. It seems every time I blink I require more spies." Yzin shook his head. "Then I taught you, myself, to read – and gave you stories which I could only hope you would glean the lessons from, of honor and strength, then pray that you would not ask Railan questions about them over me – luckily, you knew with a child's heart that that man was not safe from the beginning. I had to train you, as best I could, and hope that you would find some way to unlock your powers."

"So you ordered Joshan to –" I flushed with embarrassment, thinking of the first time I'd fucked my servant on the floor.

"Only because it was the only way. I couldn't have him fight you, could I? And yet you needed something to feel in charge of, some way to come into your own."

"I trusted you. You could have just told me."

"Would you have believed me a month ago? A year ago? Had I told you my screens were real, and the truth of the outside world?" Yzin planted a finger on his last screen. "The deeds inside those screens were real. Men and women have been dying for you to have a chance."

It felt like the room was spinning around me again. "A chance at what?"

"At really being Queen – at sweeping Railan and me and every other councilman off the board to start Aranda over again, as it should be." Yzin gave another weary sigh. "I had hoped we would have more time to train you, Ilylle. I couldn't push you, though. If I'd told you the truth before you saw your King –"

"I wouldn't have believed," I said quietly.

"And now we have little time. Tide's Day is only three days away."

Zaan stepped back, sheathing his weapon. "I must find Airelle."

Yzin groaned. "She has waited twenty-thousand years – a few days more won't matter. If we're going to succeed, we need to plan."

I watched Zaan weigh his anger against his options. He was furious at being used, and revolted at what the councilmen had done – as was I, and I had even more right to anger than him. But this was our only chance. "We have to make things right, Zaan. For everyone."

Zaan made a sound of disgust and looked to Yzin. "Promise me everyone who tortured her dies."

Yzin smiled grimly. "Everyone. Even me."

Zaan shoved his weapon back into his sheath. "What's your plan?"

I REALIZED as Yzin spoke that his plan was going to go into action with or without me. There was a machine underneath the earth ready to bore into the bottom tunnels of the palace, and men and women willing to run in through the hole it made to – up until our conversation – kill me. At the loss of their own lives. Other groups would act after that, attempting to kill off the council one by one.

I was both humbled and horrified, that they were willing to sacrifice everything – including me – to stop Railan and the rest from regenerating again.

But now that I could help, plans changed.

We would use the pretense of my ceremony to gather the entire council – I would turn Zaan back to stone, and pretend to be innocent and lure everyone in, until I released Zaan again. And then he and I would fight alongside Yzin's rebels – he would attack, and I would shield them from Railan's magic.

Yzin finished explaining and stood. "I have to leave now. Railan already fears I've grown soft. But I've made sure to do this each time, to cultivate a habit of kindliness and sorrow, so that when my iron finally strikes it will surprise him."

Each time, I thought. "How many Queens have you watched die?"

"Enough." At that, the old man finally looked away. "You must be the last, Ilylle. The world depends on it." He took my shoulders in his hands, and leaned forward to kiss the crown of my head. Then he stood and doddered down the hall.

Ilylle and I watched Rkatrayzin depart silently and all that was in me wanted to cut him down. To think he'd lived so long, so cruelly – and my Airelle –

I was startled from my thoughts by Ilylle's hand upon my arm. "Can you teach me to be a shield?"

I stared down at her. Was everything he had said true? Was she a ghost of my Airelle, come to life? I felt physically torn, between the woman I loved and the woman I wanted to hate.

I swallowed down twenty-thousand years' worth of rage. "I can," I said. "And I will. Defend –" I commanded, and pulled out my sword.

Ilylle's eyes went wide and she scooted bodily back on her couch, her skirts catching her feet as she crawled. She pointed a hand at me and I felt the heat where her magic tried to rise.

"Not attack. Defend," I said, swinging my sword at her slowly. She pointed her hand at it and it became warm.

"Defend!" I shouted, swinging at her fully. I barely stopped the sword in time, it sliced the leather around her neck but went no further.

She lay on the couch, panting in terror. "This isn't a lesson."

"You're right, it's not." I regathered myself and threw the sword aside.

In the moment my eyes left her, she bolted – flipping over and scurrying off the end of the couch to land near her chamber's doorway.

"Push me back," I commanded, striding forward.

She flung her arms out at me and I felt her will surging in the room, as my own magic protected me from the flames hers tried to light. She was pushing me, yes, but with fire – "No heat. Just intent. Quiet your emotions, and find your true strength."

I slowed so she could think on what I'd said – and then I ran straight at her. To her credit, she didn't turn and run away, but threw her arms out again.

I felt her magic catch me bodily, covering all of me like a glove. "Good. Hold it."

I thrashed inside, pushing with my own strength, and then pushing with half of my magic, slowly using it all.

"Relax," I said, and felt grounded as she released me.

"Did that work?" There was sweat at her brow, and she kneaded cramping hands.

"Yes and no. You protected yourself from me, but that's not the same as being a shield." I retrieved my dropped sword and walked over, offering it to her hilt first. "Hold this."

Ilylle shook her head. "No – I'm not good enough yet – what if –"

"I'm a Zaibann," I said, slicing through my own arm, making myself smoke in its passage.

"Okay." She laughed weakly. "Should I attack?"

"No. Just offer it out. And pretend this is real, even if it is not." I took three steps back, turned, and started walking directly at the blade.

"No no no –" she said, and threw out her other arm. The sensation of being enveloped began again as she tried to protect me from myself.

Instead of increasing up my power slowly, I slammed it at her, full force. She fell back across the floor half a step, her slippers sliding across the tile, but the sword stayed true, as did her magic.

I threw another wave at her – this time, not just force, but pain. I had pain to spare, agony for miles. Every time I hadn't felt at home in this strange world, every time I'd missed Airelle, every time I'd been forced to make do with her instead – I threw it at her.

And Ilylle, shielding me but not herself, stepped back, tears streaming from her eyes. I drew up short, and dropped my powers.

"The councilmen will use many tricks. Fire is only the most obvious weapon. They will also try to punish you with other things – fear, shame, pain. You must not only shield the rebels, but shield yourself." I reached forward and took the blade-end of the sword. She released the hilt and put her head into her hands.

"I cannot."

"You can." I tossed the sword into my other hand – and with my first, I slapped her. She looked up at me, eyes-wild. "Are you a Queen or not?"

Her jaw clenched and then her magic hit me like the blow of a thousand hammers. I was thrown back by the force of it, completely unprepared. Instinctively I rebounded and flew at her, half-man, half-smoke, reforming close.

I hit at her and she dodged, both physically and with power, leaving me lurching forward against a shield that wasn't there, pulling back to aim at me – or where she thought I was, I was too fast, letting her power slash through me then reforming again.

We fought like that, neither one landing a blow on the other, both of us too fast, looking for advantages. I had years of cunning training, but she had frightening strength. Eventually, tiring, neither one of us moved or flew, we just projected walls and inched toward the other one. I reached for her, her magic fighting mine as mine fought hers, and we grappled as though we were dancing a dance where neither of us were allowed to touch.

Sweat poured from her and she was breathing hard – I felt the same as she did but my training and my nature gave nothing away.

"Do you yield?" I asked her, on the verge of breaking down myself.

She nodded curtly rather than answer and the wall of her magic dropped. I stepped into her sphere on my own and watched her pant.

What the old man said sounded insane. But how much more proof did I need? The force I'd used against her would have killed anyone of lesser power.

"How much longer do you think you could have gone?" I asked. Her face was flush, and blood was coursing through her entire body.

"I don't know –" she caught her breath and looked down at her hands.

"Can you do that again? When lives depend on you?"

"It will be the first time I have acted like a Queen in three hundred years." She looked up at me, chin high, bearing regal. "I will do it, or I will die trying."

In that moment – she was of *her*, after all.

The binding rose in me, overpowering my sense, and without thinking I pulled her to me. One hand wrapped around her waist, the other pushed into her hair and bowed her head to one side. I could feel her power roil against me, calling like to like, her wanting me as badly as I wanted her. I lowered my head and the moment between my teeth touching her neck and piercing her tender flesh, she whispered. "And what of Airelle?"

I pulled back and my hands loosened, though need roared inside me. "Airelle is not here. Yet."

Ilylle pushed me away bodily, without power, and I let her go. She gathered herself and shook her head. "No. I want you to fuck me for me. Not because I am some available substitute. If a hole is all you want, fuck Beza." She whirled and began walking away – I caught her outstretched arm and pulled her back.

"You are the one I caught fucking the metal-beasts. Am I so easily replaced?"

She flushed bright red – and then she slapped me. I wasn't prepared for it, there was no magic behind it, or even much malice, only the warning that a line had been crossed.

"I am a Queen. I demand you treat me like one."

My jaw clenched and I stared down at her, tempted to take her blood still – only I knew if I tried to fight her now, I might not win. "As you wish, my lady," I said, and turned to walk away.

14

I stood in the hallway and watched Zaan go. I wanted him to comfort me and my body craved him – but after everything I'd found out, I needed my pride more.

I stormed into my dressing chamber and looked at myself in the mirror, leaning close enough that it fogged with my breath.

Was I real?

I might as well have been a figment of Airelle's imagination – or just another character in one of Yzin's stories. My entire world had been designed to lie to me and now that I knew the truth, what was left? I looked at my outstretched hands, as though they belonged to another. Had anything that had happened to me been mine? My people did not know me – wanted to kill me, in fact – and my King was in love with a woman from another time.

What was left for me?

Who was I?

I found I didn't really know.

I KNEW where Ilylle was inside the palace because of our bloodbond – I could feel her aimless pacing like the beating of my heart. But she didn't know where I was, and the Feather Palace was so large I could hide from her until Tide's Day – or until she used her magic to hunt me down.

Her magic. It was incredible. As a mimic of Airelle – a clone, as Yzin had said, the word cruel and unfamiliar – she was a precise one, now that her powers were untethered. If all Queens were like her, no wonder this palace was designed for placation – it wouldn't do for the pups trapped inside to realize they were wolves.

But where was the original? I had to find her to be sure.

I selfishly wanted her to be alive, so that we could be rejoined. And I selfishly wanted her dead, because if she still was alive – torture changed a man. After twenty-thousand years of torture, what of my Airelle could possibly remain?

Of course I had marked her all those years ago. I had not called on it since waking because calling and knowing nothing answered was a worse fate than never calling at all. Because her living seemed improbable – as improbable as my being bloodbound to her copy.

I stopped my own pacing and drew up short near a door. Ilylle – who wanted me, who needed me, who I had hurt because she needed it, and hurt because I wanted to hurt someone – she was right. She deserved a better King than I currently was.

Until I put my past to bed, I had no business being in hers.

It was time to call.

I walked into the nearest nexus and sat down, repeating the words in the old tongue that calmed my mind so that like could call to like again.

Airelle had a piece of me with her. It would be hers eternally, even if she had taken it to the grave.

I murmured the words under my breath, sending out wave after wave of power, hoping for even the faintest response in return. Hours passed and nothing answered me. A zoomer approached and poked me – likely to see if I needed cleaning – and I prepared to give up. I sent out a final pulse, waiting for a reply, and then opened my eyes. Airelle, in any way that I had known her, was gone.

And then I got one faint response.

Part of me wondered if it was her calling to me from across the ages – or if I'd spent so long in a trance that I'd imagined it. But another response came through, a tap of knowing, my power brushing up against my ancient trace.

"My love," I whispered, and started running down the hall.

I ran and flew, depending on how strong the signal I chased was. It faded and resurged in a slow pattern, like impossibly long breaths, and each time just as I feared I'd lost it, I would hear it again. I dove into the tunnels below the palace, down where the tunnel-beast likely was, through doors that were barred except to Zaibann smoke, and wound up in a final chamber that was cramped and small. The only light here was of my own creation – I reformed and held a flame in one hand to look around.

There was a thing that looked like Ilylle's cradle in the center of the room, inside a similar nest of wires.

"No," I whispered, walking up to it. The metal under my feet bent and broke. I put a hand on the lid, bracing for the worst, and opened it.

My flame illuminated a withered form inside. Shreds of skin over chips of bone, my love had died waiting, as I had, for a rescue that had never come. A few strands of long blonde hair, and where her neck would be, the remnants of a collar.

"No," I whispered – and the gentle force of my breath shuddered what was inside to dust – "Airelle!"

I sank to my knees beside what had become her coffin. "My love! Airelle!" I shouted her name. It echoed in the chamber, and as it began to fade, I shouted it again. I would never stop shouting it, some part of me would be screaming her name until I was placed in a grave. "Airelle!"

I crumpled forward as though struck a mortal blow and sobbed, pressing my head against the edge of the lid of the horrible thing that had killed her.

"Zaan?" a soft voice asked behind me.

I turned, eyes wet with tears, and saw the vision of my Queen – then blinked and realized it was only Ilylle, again.

"Zaan, are you okay?" She stepped into the circle of light my flame provided and looked into the coffin. "Is that –"

"My Airelle, and what they have done to her." I reached inside to touch her one more time and my fingers sifted through her dust.

"I'm so sorry, Zaan," Ilylle whispered.

"It is not how a Queen should have died – not my Queen. Scared and alone and unremembered." I was dizzy with the emotions reeling through me: vast sorrow, immense betrayal, and the violent weight of my anger. "I would go back in time and change everything."

"I know," Ilylle said. She kneeled beside me and my flame illuminated her face. Tears were streaming down it for my forgotten Queen, and that alone was what made it all right for me to cry. I sobbed and she took me in her arms.

"She died without me," I said, clinging to Ilylle's side. "I should have been there. I was meant to be there."

"It's not your fault, Zaan – you were betrayed," she said, holding me close.

"I was supposed to protect her."

Ilylle stroked her hands across my back and through my hair. "It wasn't your fault."

She was real and warm against me, my head against her shoulder, my mouth mere inches from her neck. The bloodbond roared in me again, and I needed life to come back from such profound death.

I bit her and I hung on.

She made a small noise as my teeth broke her skin. I grabbed her instinctively to keep her still – I didn't want her to jerk away and tear open her sweet flesh – and her blood began to flow inside my mouth, thick and lush. I sucked at her, rocking my tongue against the wound I'd made, making the sounds of a cornered wild animal – I needed this – she was mine – until sanity returned and I stiffened, horrified at what I'd done.

She sensed the change in me and her hand wound tight in my

hair, still offering her neck, making it all right. I carefully released her and pulled back, caution regained.

"I'm sorry."

"Don't be." My flame was extinguished and she hadn't replaced it, but I could imagine her there looking at me with her kind eyes. "This place – it's awful."

"It is." I regained control of myself and my emotions. There was something about her blood that made me feel both mortal and immortal, at the same time. "How did you get in? How did you know I was down here?"

"I heard your call, and I answered."

"I was calling Airelle."

"Yes, well –" she said in the dark, her voice small.

What was it like to discover you were just a copy? I heard the pain of it in Ilylle's voice. I put my hand out and made flame dance upon it, so that I could see her bowed head.

"But how did you get here?"

"I heard you – and you needed me. So I came."

"Teleportation?" I looked around the room, and none of the doors were open. "Ilylle, did you use your magic to transport yourself here?"

She looked up and me and nodded.

"Not even Airelle could do that."

Ilylle's expression lifted and then fell again – and I realized she was looking at the sarcophagus at my back. "Clearly."

"Clearly," I agreed. I rose and turned toward the thing again. Only the fact that Airelle was inside it stopped me from tearing it apart. "That they would do this – to her – to others like her – without consequences for so long –"

"It has to end with me, Zaan." Her voice was grim. I looked down to find her brow drawn in an unfamiliar line and her chest was heaving – not with pain from the bite I'd inflicted, but with anger. "They cannot do this again. Not to anyone else."

"They won't. I swear it." I offered her my hand to help stand up and she took it, sealing our pact. She stood, her hair wild from our prior fight, and while the wound I'd made was healing, her neck and collar were still stained with blood.

In that moment she was the image of Airelle, so close it took my breath away, then she moved and she was Ilylle again, proud and kind.

"How do I get back?" she asked.

"Wait until my return, and I'll call." I was phasing into smoke, but retook form more solidly. "This time, my call will be for you."

She nodded.

I let myself go incorporeal, faded around Ilylle, and sank into Airelle's tomb again, blowing through her remains, suffusing myself with her, whispering the old words, "This is not a good-bye, but a parting," before flowing over the lip of the coffin and underneath the door.

WITH THE POWER of Ilylle's blood I traversed the palace quickly and reformed inside her chamber, not far away from Joshan. I could feel Ilylle in the dungeon Airelle was left in, and this time I called for her, like to like, the woman I was bloodbound to. I pulled on the piece of her tethered to me – and felt her pull shiver through my body as she answered back. Then a moment of blankness, and she reformed at my side.

"My Queen," I said with a nod.

She flicked a hand along her blood-stained dress, a low imitation of a curtsy. "My King."

Joshan was apparently unperturbed at two different people reforming nearby, but at seeing Ilylle he broke into a wide smile. "My Queen, the dream cradle awaits."

Ilylle stood still with horror.

"No," I answered him. I could see it there, the disgusting implement they'd used to enslave Airelle – no Queen of mine was ever getting into one again. I drew up power inside myself and crossed the room to ruin the device.

"Hold," Ilylle said from behind me.

"You know what it is. What it does. I will not let you get into it." Ilylle's looked almost exactly like Airelle's. Of course it did, why change something that clearly worked? I could destroy it with a blow, a kick, a thought –

"If we destroy it, they'll know."

I looked back at her. "Let the fight begin now, Ilylle –"

"It's been almost two days. They expect me to use it. We have to keep up pretense." She walked around me and put herself between me and the cradle.

"Are you insane? What if –"

"I know what if," she said calmly. "I saw her too." But she put one foot into the cradle nonetheless. "This is what I have to do, Zaan. Lives are depending on me."

"People you don't even know –" I protested.

"My people, nonetheless."

I walked up to her, ready to snatch her out of the cradle at the slightest sign. What moved in me now wasn't just the bond of our blood but something deeper and more intense. "I, also, depend on you."

She gave me the softest saddest smile, and in that moment looked almost exactly like Airelle had when she first suggested that my people turn to stone. "And I, you. So please stand guard," she said, and lay down in the cradle, bringing its lid down.

I PACED a line in front of the cradle. Could I have gotten into it, after seeing my Airelle? I didn't think I could. But she had. Like a man walking onto a gallows, or off a plank in the middle of the sea. Railan's men could be here in moments, with another magic-eater to disrupt me and lash the lid of that beast down, with her trapped inside its belly.

She had to have known the risks and accepted them. Why had I ever spent so much time hating her when she was capable of this? So eager to find flaws with her, comparing her to Airelle, that I couldn't see all the ways she was alike?

And yet different, too – Ilylle was her own being. She had done the best with what she had, and had come so far, so bravely, in such a short time. I sat down on the ground, with my back to her cradle. Anything that wanted to hurt her would literally have to go through me.

"Beza, bring me a meal."

"Yes, my King," the metal-puppet said.

I crossed my legs and waited for dinner or death, whichever came first.

15

Time passed as I paced around the cradle. Longer than I liked. The colors on Ilylle's walls ebbed and flowed like the tide, mimicking the passage of light outdoors, day into night and back again.

Had she ever been in this long before? How could she stand it? Was she all right? I didn't need to sleep to have nightmares, every time I blinked I imagined opening up the lid of her cradle to find her drained to dust inside.

My poor Airelle – her pride was another way she and Ilylle were alike. How could she have let herself be tormented for so long? Why hadn't she killed herself when she'd had the chance?

Everyone with magic was able to point it inward – it was one of the burdens of the power, always knowing how easy it was to burn yourself away with it. I knew Airelle wasn't afraid of pain – which left me with a horrific realization.

Airelle knew if she died there'd be no one left to save me.

I was the reason she'd been trapped. She must have hoped beyond hope that someday she'd find a way free and rescue me. Hours, months, years, spent inside that monstrosity – I couldn't let the same thing happen to Ilylle.

She would have to turn me into stone again for Yzin's plan to work – and I would have to convince her to leave me there, if it meant saving herself.

I could not lose two Queens in one lifetime.

THIS TIME, I remembered my dreams. I was swirling with power, sinking in a boat at sea, drowning, water on all sides pressing in.

When I woke I flung the lid of the cradle back and gulped in air. Zaan rushed to my side and pulled me out with a stricken expression on his face, setting me carefully on my bed. "Are you all right?"

I looked down at myself and then nodded slowly. "I...think so. I feel very weak though – how much time passed?"

"Too long. Tide's Day is tomorrow." Everything about him was serious – his face, his bearing. He'd sat outside the cradle for two days, standing guard, preparing for a threat that hadn't come, coping with the loss of his love.

"Oh," I breathed, and got my bearings. I had never been in the cradle that long before. Had Railan been trying to drain the last bit of strength from me? One last time to stop me from finding my true potential out? "Is – is everyone ready?"

"I don't know. Yzin hasn't returned and I haven't left your side."

"Thank you," I said with a slight nod.

"You're welcome." His gaze traveled over all of me. "Are you well?"

"I'm whole. Just weak." I hugged myself and ran my hands up and down my arms.

"We have time to make you strong."

His voice was flat when he said it, with no undertone of anticipation, but he reached for the buckles of his armor. I hadn't seen his chest since he'd proved Beza unreal to me – I watched him take off the layers of leather bracings and pull the shirt underneath off over his head. He stayed standing at the far end of the bed, his expression stern – like he was trapped in stone again already. I rose up and crawled over to him, reaching out a tentative hand out to trace one of his scars.

"How did you get this?"

He looked down, following the movement of my hand. "It's one of the incentives to learn how to transform – eventually you'd rather become smoke than have a priest beat you again."

"That sounds awful."

"It was at the time. It served its purpose, though." His head was bowed and his hands went for the buckles at his waist.

"And your armor? How does it transform with you –" I asked, my voice rising nervously. He stopped unbuckling things and pierced me with a look, and I rocked back, scooting incrementally away. "Are you mad at me?"

His expression softened for a moment and then drew tight. "I just want to make you strong again, Ilylle." He mounted the bed and pushed the rest of his armor down, revealing a swelling cock. "If there is a time for kindness, when all this is through, then I can afford to be. But for now –" he reached forward to take the hem of my dress up in both hands and pulled, making the fabric tear up in a jagged line. "You will have to make due with what I can give you."

Then he reached up the bed, grabbed my hips, and pulled me down to him. Our legs were tangled for a moment until he'd put one of mine on either side of his thighs. He hovered over me, holding himself up on his arms, looking angrily down.

I'm not sure what I was then – my magic swirled inside me, making me ache, but I was scared.

Zaan leaned forward, his face directly over mine. "If the choice comes down to me or you, promise me you'll save yourself."

I shook my head without thinking. "No."

"Promise me," he growled, "or I won't let you turn me back to stone and all is lost."

I grit my teeth together. "That's not fair."

"I am not kind nor fair today then." He reached and wound one hand in my hair tight, taking control of my head, sending electric shivers of good-pain-fear down my spine. "Promise me."

If I couldn't turn him back to stone, none of Yzin's plan would work. More people would die, the councilmen would still live, and they would do this to another girl. "I promise," I gasped out, as the pain made my eyes water.

"Good," Zaan said, and set to fucking me.

His knees pushed my thighs out and his hips lowered and his cock pushed against the entrance of my pussy. He took one of my hands, and then the other, holding them down with one of his over my head so that I couldn't struggle with him.

I wouldn't have. I needed him again. Being in the same room with him, muchless the same bed, raked the embers of magic inside me, and I could feel the strength I'd lost to the cradle rebuilding. He reached down to angle himself to take me, as I tilted my hips up, begging him to push in – and then he stopped, leaning back and releasing my wrists.

"I'm sorry – I forgot – you've only been with the puppet – "

"And you, once. When you were stone." I pushed myself up on my elbows, heart racing, breathing hard. "Whatever you need to do to me, Zaan, I can take it."

My Zaibann warrior made a strangled sound, and leaned back in.

His cock was in me in a moment as his body curved and I cried out at feeling him slide home, hard. There was something about the way he filled me – like Joshan never had – or maybe it was all the sensations that came with it, knowing he needed me, that he craved my blood – within thrusts, I gathered my feet under my knees so that I could thrust back, taking his cock each time it was given.

He kissed me roughly and I felt his fangs scratch my tongue and scrape my lips – it was like he was devouring me, but it was all right, because I needed him just as badly. I held onto his back, felt the ripple and curve of his muscles there, reached down to grab his ass to feel him thrust into me, and then freed myself of his mouth to start kissing him back, tasting as much of him as I could, his chin, his neck, his shoulder, biting him for all the times he'd bitten me, listening to the low groans rumbling through his body every time his cock rowed forward.

If I rocked my hips just right I could rub myself against him more, and soon with each thrust there was a hiccup of time where I ground against him hard. I felt my magic tighten in my belly, in my chest, as one of his hands kneaded my breast and he leaned down to suck my nipple hard. I started to moan and my body started to do what it needed to, hungry on its own, my hips bobbing faster, rubbing harder against him. Zaan groaned again and looked down at me with dark eyes.

"Keep it. Keep it in you. Don't let it out."

I knew what he meant – I tried to hold onto the magic as it fought me for control, wanting to come out of me in a screaming rush.

"You can do it, Ilylle. Be its master," he said, without relenting.

"Za-an –" His name broke in my throat and my hands clenched over his shoulders and my hips sprang up and held there, taking all of his cock in and rubbing against him. "Zaan, yes – Zaan!" I bit my own lip then shouted his name again. "Zaan!"

He made low growling sounds at this, continuing to fuck me through. My power whirled out of me for an uncontrolled instant – and then just as quickly flew back in. I shuddered beneath him, quaking, feeling ecstatic and divine.

"Good, Ilylle," he murmured, pushing my hair out of my face. "Good." He took two more strokes in me, and then pulled out.

I was too dizzy to realize what had happened for a moment, as he started put his armor back on. Then I realized – "Wait – you –"

"When you turn me into stone, I have to be hard."

"No –" I shook my head. I was strong now – I didn't need the fucking anymore, but I didn't want to be left like this. "Zaan –"

He stopped and looked at me. "What was your first lesson?"

I thought back quickly. "To take what I want, or be content with what I'm given."

He nodded, fastening another buckle. "Are you not content?"

"No." I rose up in bed, pulling the rest of my poor torn dress off, crawling over to him. If he would not put his seed inside me, I would suck it out of him again. My power swirled around me, crackling like electricity. I could make him fuck me again, I knew it.

He watched me, his eyes traveling over my body as I neared. When I was close enough to touch, he put his hand out, trailing his fingers through the veil of my hair. "If you do that you will break me, Ilylle."

I sat back abashed, as he continued to pull on his clothes. His actions were deliberate, familiar, but I could read the tension in him. Just as I had had to conquer the cradle, he would have to conquer being remade stone. He finished the last buckle, and I reached for my dress, hopping off my bed.

"Stay naked. It makes it easier for me to stay this way."

"If it helps you." I leaned in and kissed him. His armor was cold, the buckles and leather made my nipples light up, and I felt his cock rub against me as I rose up on my toes.

He breathed heavily as I rocked back. "That helps, too. Let's go."

We walked back to his display chamber. Neither one of us had been back since he'd bitten me, although the zoomers had moved all the furniture, preparing for the ceremony. All the seats were arranged in rows at the back half of the room, with an isle down the center that we walked down until we reached his empty pedestal.

Zaan stepped up onto it. "How did I look?"

"Worried. A little angry. Kind of like now." I reached up and pushed his braid to hang down his back.

"You've got to shield yourself from them, Ilylle. If they know how powerful you are now, they'll never come near you, they'll kill you from afar. Keep your power hidden at all times – pretend to be the girl you were when I first met you here."

I looked around, imagining who I used to be. So much had happened since then. I might as well have been a copy when I'd first fucked him, idiotic and innocent – I knew so much more now. "I'm not like her anymore."

"I know. But you must not let on."

I frowned but still answered, "I promise."

"I've marked where Yzin's soldiers will enter –" he said, and held his hand out to me. I took it, and felt the passing of a piece of knowledge – the sensation of being called from deep in the Feather Palace's halls. "When they breech the wall, you'll have to protect them until they get up here to help fight."

"I will."

A moment of silence passed between us as we both contemplated our difficult paths, and then Zaan reached down to stroke himself with a sigh. "I can't believe I was displayed like this."

"I'm the one who has to fuck you in front of all of them," I said, stepping close. He grimaced and shook his head.

"It'd better be you when I wake again, Ilylle."

"It will be." I pushed his hand out of the way and replaced it with my own. He was soft – because unlike Joshan he was mortal and knew fear. I leaned in, as his hands took the position they'd held for centuries when he was a statue. "The next time you see me..." My voice drifted, search for words. "I'll be right in front of you – when you wake up, I'll be the first thing you see. You'll feel me wrapped around you, and you'll know that I am yours and you are mine."

My Zaibann's chest heaved and emotions raced across his face – sympathy, longing, need – and his cock firmed in my hand. "Ilylle," he whispered, as I wished that stiffness through his entire body, for him to be bereft of life as I knew it, to change back into a statue. I closed my eyes and willed it as I kept stroking – and when I realized I was rubbing stone I opened my eyes again.

It had worked. I was alone inside the Feather Palace once more.

"This is not a good-bye, but a parting," I whispered, and stepped back.

16

"Am I doing something wrong, my Queen?"

I shook my head. "No, Beza. Just keep going."

There'd been a time in my life when I'd looked forward to ceremonial baths – the endless quantities of oils that Beza poured on me and then scraped off, the way her fingers massaged between my muscles, slipping over every inch of skin.

If I were still the naive girl I'd been mere days ago, I'd be twisting and turning inside Beza's embrace, whispering my foolish hopes into her unreal ears. But now, knowing all? Each bath was intolerable, and each touch burned like flame.

I pulled on the simple white silk dress I was supposed to sleep in somehow, and entered my bed. Either the zoomers or Joshan had straightened the sheets after my last encounter with Zaan – there was nothing that proved he'd ever been here at all, except for my memories.

I tugged the sheets up as the lights in the chamber dimmed – and a man appeared in the hallway.

I leaped up, Zaan's name on my lips – just as he strode in, and I realized it was Railan.

"My Queen," he said, by way of announcement.

"High Councilman," I responded, clutching my sheets up to my neck. When was the last time Railan had come by personally? Was he going to wrestle me into the cradle again?

"I'm sorry to startle you," he said with a bow, before walking in to sit at the edge of my bed. "I just wanted to see with my own eyes that you were ready." I felt his power snaking around the room, pressing in. It was hard not to let my magic flare in indignant response – but I remembered my promise in time.

"I can't wait," I said, feigning breathlessness. "I feel like I've waited my whole life for this day."

Railan chuckled, his power receding. "Indeed you have. You have no idea, my Queen, just how magical tomorrow will be."

When a group of men would be standing nearby waiting to watch me die. I kept my smile plastered on and was grateful for the lowered lights. "Tell me about it?" I begged him.

He shook his head. "There's no way to explain it, Ilylle. It's an experience you just have to go through." He stood and looked at me and I wondered how many Queens he had looked at in the past, just like this, hungering for their lives. "Good-night, my Queen. I look forward to seeing you tomorrow."

"And I, you," I said, still smiling. *But not the way you think.*

I MANAGED to sleep at the end of the night, but Beza woke me early to work on pinning up my hair. The celestians had sent a dress for me – it was gold and absolutely lovely, the kind of dress I would adore if I hadn't known I was meant to die with it on. Soon singing started in the Zaibann Chamber, and other servants came into my dressing room.

"Happy Tide's Day, my Queen," said a blonde as she entered, and it was echoed by a brunette by her side.

"And happy Tide's Day to you," I responded to both of them.

"You look lovely, my Queen," said the brunette.

"Thank you," I said. Neither of them were real either, but they set to helping Beza straighten out the hem of my gown, after lacing me into exquisitely gilded shoes, and then they all fussed over setting gemstones into my hair, and brought out jeweled bracelets for my wrists and arms.

I caught sight of myself in the mirror when they were through. I looked like a creature made of gold and glass – I closed my eyes as they powdered my cheeks and reddened my lips.

"We're finished, my Queen," the blonde announced. "Are you ready?"

I inhaled and exhaled deeply. I was so close to seeing Zaan again – everything would be all right if I just focused on that. "Yes."

"I'm so glad, my Queen," the brunette enthused. She offered me her hand and I took it, walking with her in the unfamiliar heeled shoes they'd put me in, into my own chamber, where a crew of male servants – Joshan included – stood on either side of some sort of strange chair.

"What is that?" I asked before I could help myself – but surely asking some questions was normal.

"It's your wedding throne, my Queen," the blonde said, smiling eagerly.

I had a throne. This did not look like one. It looked molded for my body, with holes at intervals on its edges. "And I'm supposed to sit in it?"

"Yes, my Queen. It's part of the ceremony," said the brunette. I looked to Beza and saw neither confirmation nor denial.

Did Railan know? Was that chair some way to trap me and put me into the cradle again? There was no way of knowing – there was only going through.

"If you will, my Queen," the brunette said, pulling me gently. I went with her and pretended not to care.

Once I'd sat on the 'throne', the remaining servants looped gold chains through the holes to lash me down at my chest and waist, while the ones at my ankles were hidden by my dress.

"Are you ready, my Queen?" the blonde asked, as the singing down the hall took on a fevered pitch.

"Yes," I answered calmly, fighting to keep my magic down.

The servants started singing and wheeled my throne out of my chambers, down the hall to where I'd left Zaan.

I knew the words to the song as they pushed me, and knew too that I ought to be singing along at this point, at my pleasure at meeting my true King at last, and how lovely it was going to be to be paired with him, ruling Aranda side-by-side.

I moved my mouth but no words came out. What if I couldn't turn Zaan back? What if I did, and the room was full of more cradles, and both of us died? I felt my power begin to swell in me in my panic, then remembered to press it back down, forcing myself to sing a few notes. Beza was walking beside me, and Joshan somewhere behind – I wanted them to stay close, but didn't think it was safe.

"Joshan, Beza, wait for me in my room, will you? I'll be back soon."

"Of course, my Queen," they both answered at once, and bowed away from my 'throne'.

The other servants kept singing as we walked through the doorway. My council was arrayed three rows deep in an even arc away from Zaan, and they turned to watch me enter as my new throne was pushed down the aisle. Some of them had tears streaming down their cheeks – for me? For my fate? No, I realized as I looked around, my elaborate hair crunching on the throne's back behind me – they were crying with relief for themselves, that my death would invigorate them again. I sought out Yzin instinctively. He wasn't crying and I kept his gaze for as long as I could, until the servants pushed me past.

Railan stood in front of Zaan, in his red robes with their gold flying lilans, holding a book. The song was almost done now and somehow I'd managed to keep singing, out of years of habit and foolish hope. When it finished Railan made a gesture and the servants brought me near. It was impossible to look at Zaan and not think of all we'd done, the time we'd spent – my magic wanted to flare, but I pushed it down.

"Ilylle, Queen of Dreams, you have served Aranda long and well," Railan said, smiling graciously. "It is time that you take your reward in the arms of your Zaibann King, who you will rule with side by side forevermore."

Railan leaned forward and picked up my skirts, pulling them high, as the throne tilted precipitously back. I gasped, both at being jolted and exposed.

"I am sorry the manner of your wedding has been withheld from you till now, but you will come to understand things quickly enough," he said. Servants spun wheels on either side of me, and the throne I was lashed to split apart at the thighs, pulling one leg to either side, as other wheels propped the whole thing up, so that Zaan and I were almost level.

Railan reached into a pocket of his robe and pulled out a jar, unscrewing its lid, to dip in his fingers. He slicked something on Zaan's cock, and then pressed his hand to my dark place, greasing me there. I gasped as he leaned forward. "My final kindness to you, my unwedded Queen." He waved his other hand and the song started up again, as he walked back out of sight.

Servants on either side started rowing the throne forward, as others spun more wheels, all the better to align my pussy with Zaan's cock. As much as I wanted him to be alive again, I didn't want it like this – with singing servants on either side, and all of the council waiting at my back. I closed my eyes and bit my lip and tried not to gasp as his coldness pressed in.

His name was on my lips but I managed not to say it. I tilted myself as the servants rowed me fractionally back and forth, my dark place taking more of his cock in each time. He was so hard now it hurt, but that didn't matter – what mattered was getting him inside me, so that together our magic would flow out.

"My King," I said, as the servants pushed me forward again, and I winced. "My love –" I whispered, only for him, on their next thrust.

With a final push, we sealed, his chill cock settled inside and I squeezed it tight with my dark place, just as I'd told him I would.

"Zaan, live," I whispered, and let my magic burst out.

Color returned to him in an instant, and he sagged forward against my throne. They'd aligned that part perfectly, his mouth fell against my neck, and I felt the heat of his warm breath. "Is it you?" I felt more than heard him say.

"It is," I answered just as low.

He bit down then, and I gasped, pulling at him inside of me. He leaned on the throne and took two more thrusts, while filling himself with my blood. I could almost hear the councilmen waiting for the moment of my death, imagining them leaning forward in their seats – as Zaan raked his hands through the chains at my side, freeing me.

"Let's show them how we will rule, my Queen," he said, pulling back and out of me, lips stained with my blood in a cruel smile, before turning into smoke.

17

I heard the sounds of the battle begin behind me before I could turn. I leaned forward to undo the chains at my ankles, as the heads of servants rolled on the ground – I could see the metal inside, just like Zaan said there'd be – and he'd already winnowed half the first row of councilmen – soon the heads of Jallisan, Oinan, and Bronan rolled on the ground beside their slaves.

I leapt down from the throne, turned towards the room, and Railan's power buffeted me like a wall. "You were supposed to die, girl!"

The force of it stunned me and I staggered back until I hit the pedestal where Zaan had been. Feeling its cold stone behind me reminded me of all he'd done to others of my kind – I unleashed a torrent of rage at him. It twinkled in the air between us like fire.

"I hate you!" I screamed.

His surprise was evident on his face as he tried to stand against my onslaught. Zaan's mercilessness continued, disappearing and reappearing to crush skulls and break necks.

"My people are through, Ilylle! Shield them!" Yzin shouted. Others of his kind realized his deception and fell on him as he stepped back.

I sought out Zaan's marker with my mind, until I saw a group of men and women in my mind, surrounded by waist-high zoomers, the size that'd moved Zaan's statue. Their paws opened up and instead of dusters and sewing implements, weaponry came out, and they began lashing bullets at them.

I screamed in horror – and flung a hand out. In an instant, they were covered in a bubble of safety, though I could feel every time the bullets hit my wall.

"Ilylle!" Zaan said, reforming near me.

"Keep fighting!" I commanded, and he disappeared again.

Railan lifted his hands to the ceiling. "I'm not losing twenty-thousand years of life to you –" he shouted, and it started raining fire.

I threw a shield out to protect myself, feeling divided – it was like one of my eyes watched the growing chaos around me as the councilmen fought against Zaan, while the other watched Yzin's people struggle against the zoomers. Their progress was slow – the zoomers were relentless, as was Railan's onslaught – without thinking about it, I pulled them *here*.

They reformed in the middle of the chamber, their own weapons out, still under the protection of my shield. In seconds, bullets ricocheted around the room.

Up until that moment, the council hadn't realized they were fighting for their lives. Surprised by the change of events and weakened from waiting for my power, they'd responded slowly – but now I felt them attacking me. A wall of wind rushed through the room and put Railan's fires out, but took all the air with it, trying to choke me – I fought back and forced the room to breathe. Intolerable heat welled up from the ground, and set the throne on fire, but I changed my shield to keep Yzin's fighters cool, as decapitated servant bodies melted on the ground.

Everything slowed. All I could manage was defense as tidal waves of magic buffeted the room. I wasn't fast enough once and a soldier's arm vaporized outside my protection – she screamed, as I screamed at seeing it – and all my walls wavered.

"Keep going!" Yzin ordered from his corner of the room, where two councilmen beset him. They were pressing in and –

"No!" I shouted as one of them sheathed a knife in Yzin's stomach. "No! No! No!"

The room became electrified around me. The bodies that remained all flew up, as did the councilmen and soldiers, everyone that was left inside the chamber. "No!" I shouted, putting an end to anyone's magic still inside the room. Everyone, everything, dropped. The soldiers recovered before the few remaining councilmen did, and fell on them. The sounds of gunshot echoed in the chamber and rang down all the Feather Palace's halls, as I ran to Yzin's side. "Let me heal you –" I fell to kneeling and reached for his wound.

Zaan reformed beside me in a moment, placing his hand on my shoulder.

Yzin grunted. "Don't worry. I remember my promise, Zaibann. I wouldn't have gone through with this if I wasn't prepared to die."

"But – it's not fair –" I began.

"It is. No one should live as long as I have." Yzin looked past me. "Elissa!"

The soldier whose arm had been vaporized stepped up – her other arm still held a metal gun. So many things I had only read about, only to now see them all. "The men taking Railan's compound haven't checked in yet, Sir."

Yzin made another groaning sound, this time in anger. "Is he dead?" I looked around the carnage of the room, the pools of metal, blood, and ash. I couldn't tell what was what anymore, but I felt inside my bones that he was not among their number.

"No. I marked him while we were fighting," Zaan said, before I could voice my concern. "I can feel him moving –"

Yzin's face went whiter. "Both of you, go after him now – I'm sure he has backup plans – if he wakes and kills another clone, it just might be enough –"

Zaan stepped back, half of him twisting to smoke. "I can't take you my way."

I put my hand out for Zaan's and caught it before he changed. "But I can take you mine. Show me where to go."

My King looked from my hand to me and then I felt the knowledge of his marker wash in.

18

W e reappeared together inside a metal hall. Zaan went to smoke in an instant and I whirled to look at our surroundings.

The walls were lined with what looked like human-sized jars. And in each of them was a different version of me. Some of them were half-formed, others floating groups of organs held together by tenuous tissue, and still others looked ready to breathe.

I spun, surrounded by horrors.

"Do you grasp your true nature now, my Queen?" Railan taunted, his voice piped in overhead. I couldn't feel his marker anymore, I didn't know where he was. "And you thought you could trace me, Zaibann? Please. I have not forgotten your skills since the time I saw you last."

Zaan reformed beside me, his expression dark. "You need to get out of here, Ilylle. Go back."

"Not until everything inside this room is destroyed." I threw my power against the nearest glass jar. It cracked, and a lifeless girl who looked like me slid out in a rush of foul smelling liquid.

"How will you control Aranda, Ilylle?" Railan taunted. His voice traveled now, as though he were walking the perimeter of the room.

"You're just a concept, a name. No one's ever seen you – there's even a religion that posits that you don't exist. That's how little you matter to them."

"I will rule better than you have!" I shattered another glass, and organs unspooled onto the floor.

"How do you know? Because Yzin told you so? That ignorant fool?"

"Come out and fight me, Railan!" Zaan yelled.

"Why should I, when I don't have to?" Railan said, and around us, machinery thrummed. The same sound I heard-felt when I stepped into the dream-cradle, just as it turned on. "How do you think I keep them all docile and waiting?"

"Ilylle!" Zaan warned, before turning to smoke.

"No!" I surged my power out and shook the walls, and the vats around me broke with the force of it, gallons of fluid and tissues souping the floor. But past that, the cradle-apparatus ate my power up, and kept draining. My anger created a vast power inside of me, but it wasn't endless well. "Zaan –" I turned, looking for him to regather, but he was still gone. "Zaan?"

The door in front of me opened, revealing Railan standing inside. "My disruptor ate your Zaibann – and you won't be far behind."

It felt like it was cutting the parts of me that were most *me* out with a hot blade – or maybe that was just the loss of Zaan. "How will you live forever without me – without them?" I gestured to the remnants of all the other clones on the floor.

"I can make a few other girls easily enough. Harvest them young, now that I'm only feeding myself," he said with a shrug. He made a gesture, the thrumming got louder, and I fell to my knees in the gory slush.

"And Aranda?" I asked, trying to hold parts of *myself* in.

"We'll use old images of you. No one need ever know the truth, not for another hundred years."

"Someone will find out the truth. Someone will stop you."

"Once you're gone, my Queen, no one will know." He made another gesture and the disruptor's onslaught doubled. I fell face down in the sloshing liquid, utterly bereft of strength. I closed my eyes, exhaled my last breath and inhaled wetly, fully expecting to drown.

Instead, I found that I could breathe. I floated in the waters, buoyed up just as my stillborn sisters had been, suspended inside all of their jars. I wondered what this strange liquid surrounding me was – blood, birthing fluid, tears? Whatever it was sheltered me now, holding me safe and protected like a hand.

I'd taken my own life for granted for three hundred years – and then I'd complained and fought against it. My sisters here had never had that chance, half-formed, stunted, trapped by Railan. But I could feel them striving as they wrapped around me, trying to *become*.

I was enveloped in a slow moving consciousness that was abundantly me. Everything around me a part of myself – and I was a piece of all of it. I gave myself over to it, and together we were more powerful than Railan could have ever imagined.

"Sisters, come," I willed into the water, and they answered me. Arms and legs, livers and hearts, a slurry of everything that could have been Airelle or Ilylle, and everything that never was – skin and tissue and bone pressing together, joining.

I would have thought that it would hurt, but instead it felt like coming home.

Welcome.

Welcome.

Welcome.

Things sparked. Hearts beat. Muscles moved. Blood flowed.

We formed into something absolutely other that was still precisely who we were – possessed of one wide body, six arms, eight legs, and twenty beating hearts. We rose from the murk as one as Railan sank back in horror.

"Railan, you have eons of evil to answer for," three voices spoke from three separate heads, and I didn't know or care which one was mine.

"How can you – what are you –" His voice rose in panic. The thrumming of the disruptor increased, I felt it buffeting the outer layers of our skin, but we were too much for it. With all our powers combined we were the endless well that would never be drained – and before he could close the door, we crawled up the stairs to drag him down to our level.

The disruptor's full force hit him and he screamed, dwindling before our eyes. "Off! Off!" he shouted, and his hidden machinery obeyed.

"We are Airelle," we told him as one.

"No – you're dead – you all should be dead!" he said, thrashing inside our six-armed grasp.

"The one who should be dead is you," we said, and started to pull.

"Ilylle!" Zaan reformed beside us as he shouted our name.

We hesitated and looked down, and I saw Zaan through six different eyes. "You live," I said, and my single heart thrilled to see him.

"I do," he said, looking up at what I currently was, mystified. "Because of your blood in me. The disruptor tried to pull me apart, but I knew where I belonged. You were my anchor."

"She's a monster now, Zaibann, surely you can see that! The thing you love has become the creature I feared!" Railan shouted, as he struggled in our grasp.

"You are what we have feared, for twenty-thousand years," we said, and began to squeeze again.

"No," Zaan shook his head, putting his hand on my nearest arm. "Not like this. Killing him is too easy. You know what we need to do." He gave me a knowing look, and I remembered Airelle, my progenitor, myself.

"Yes," we answered, with three separate mouths. We wheeled the bulk of our body back and crawled up through the door into the next room with Railan still in our arms. Halfway up he gathered our intent.

"No – do not – I beg of you –" He twisted his head back. "Zaibann, this is not all of them – I kept a pure cell line, I've been holding it in reserve, should the copies degenerate. I could make the very image of your Airelle – she'd be the most perfect copy I've ever done – like your love in word, in thought, in deed! If you kill me, she dies as well, forgotten anew!" His voice rose and broke as he pleaded, and beside us Zaan stiffened. "All you have to do is kill the monster!" Railan shrieked.

We looked at our King. He disappeared to smoke in an instant. Railan thought he'd won and brayed his triumph – and then the disruptor in the clone room thrummed back on, as Zaan reformed again at our side.

"There is no more Airelle. You killed her," Zaan said.

We threw Railan into the room, and slammed shut the door.

19

If I wasn't Airelle, who was I? I felt infinitely expansive and yet also minutely small – as though I had lived for eons smashed inside an instant.

"Ilylle," Zaan said, looking up at us with concern.

"Shhhh," we advised from our three throats, as everything began to loosen. Seams shifted, skin parted, organs, muscles, bones moved. I condensed, folding in pieces of my sisters from all around me, shrinking in and focused, until I resembled myself again, settling on the two legs and arms that were my own, stepping out of the sloughed skin of my sisters like a newborn.

Zaan's eyes widened, watching me transform. "You are more powerful than you know."

"No," I told him. "I know exactly how powerful I am now." Pieces of me had been waiting for this moment for twenty thousand years, and I would carry them with me forevermore. "Shall we finish?"

Zaan nodded.

Together we started enough fires that Railan's palace looked like a sun – or so I assumed since when we exited it was night.

. . .

I PULLED us back to the Feather Palace and together we reformed. Yzin's body was the only one intact, the soldiers had placed it on Zaan's old pedestal. Seeing him, I rushed to his side, and the soldiers moved back for me.

"He's dead, my Queen," Elissa said in a somber tone.

The only person who'd ever tried to help me for the first three hundred years of my life. I wound my hand through the bloody fabric of his robe. "Did he know before he died that his plan worked?"

"Who can say?" she answered truthfully.

Zaan put a hand on my shoulder. "He died knowing he'd tried. That's more than most men get."

I swallowed back tears, and stood. The soldiers gawked at me, and I looked down. My gold dress was covered in gore, and there were streaks of red staining my arms – they'd only ever seen me looking perfect on their screens. I wondered what they thought of me now.

"You...mentioned healing him earlier," Elissa went on, and gestured to the bloody stump of her arm, capped with crude gauze.

"Of course. Take that off."

A few days ago seeing her wound would have made me ill, but now – I concentrated and waved my hand, willing her to knit. She closed her eyes and sucked in air as though it hurt – but when she dared opened them again, her arm was whole.

"You really are a Queen," she said in awe.

"I know." The way she looked at me now – would everyone in Aranda look at me like that? I wasn't sure how that made me feel. "And the rest of Yzin's plan? Are we in control?"

"Of all the strategic locations and networks – but we don't have enough people to hold them indefinitely. The council had followers, and Aranda has no shortage of opportunists interested in power for their own." She made a face and cleared her throat. "If I may, my Queen –"

"Ilylle. Anyone in this room may always call me Ilylle."

"Yzin left a set of instructions – suggestions, really."

Zaan snorted and I smiled. "Bring them to me. My King and I will give them the consideration they deserve."

"Thank you...Ilylle," she said, catching herself. "And, until then?"

I looked around the room. Zaan was at my side, but he knew no more of the world outside than I did – there was so much to learn. But one question needed answering first. "Does Aranda really want a ruler?"

"Even if it doesn't, it needs one for a time."

"Should that ruler be me?" I asked. Her eyes widened enormously.

"Yzin vouched for you. He said that you would rule wisely and fair – and you'd have enough power to get us through the chaos of being reborn."

"Do you agree?" I asked.

She nodded and looked to her fellow soldiers, who nodded too. Then she gave me a nervous grin. "He also said you'd have enough sense to leave government when it was time."

"Good. I will be a Queen for life, it is who I am. But being a Queen does not mean I have to be a ruler. I won't have you trade their shackles for mine." I inhaled and exhaled deeply. "I need a moment to gather myself. Today has been long."

"Word will get out, my Queen," one of the men said. "Everyone will know by dawn –"

"Good. Tell them to expect me then. I'll make an appearance." I looked down at myself. I would bathe and change dresses between now and then, but I was ready to be clean now. I swept my hands over myself and off again, and all the blood I'd been covered in went with the motion, leaving only fabric and my skin behind.

"Where?" Elissa asked.

"In my reception chamber. I'll open the doors to the stairs –"

The man nodded but made a strained face. "But there are no stairs into the palace –"

"There will be once I make them," I said. His eyebrows rose, and he nodded his head and bowed both at once.

"That's enough for now. Dawn will be here fast enough," Zaan said, catching my hand. I looked to it, and then to him, and saw him looking down. My heart swelled. After all this time, so much hoping and waiting – this was what it felt like to have a King standing by my side.

"Joshan – Beza!" I called, and my two loyal servants appeared. I gestured at the soldiers. "Treat them to all the pleasures the Feather Palace has to offer. Bathe them, feed them, show them all the halls, except for my great chamber."

"And the reception hall," Zaan added.

The palace was big enough, I shrugged and smiled, adding, "And then bring them back at dawn."

Elissa looked over at me, a question on her face. "I am not greeting a land of strangers on my own," I explained.

The expression she wore then flickered from worried to mystified – and then wound up on hope. I could see it in her eyes, and the way she smiled when she raised her chin.

Beza took the nearest soldier's hand. "If I may," she began, leading him out.

"This way," Joshan said to the rest, gesturing grandly behind her.

Looking nervously to one another, the soldiers followed them out into the hall – and one by one we heard them whooping and congratulating one another on surviving. Zaan turned to me when the echoes of their delight had faded away.

"Do you think that's wise?" he asked.

"Why wouldn't it be?"

"They'll see the luxury you've been living in here, while they've been struggling outside."

"I intend on sharing my luxury with them. And fixing Aranda – once I understand it. I expect that will take some time." I'd only seen the smallest piece of it from the burning roof of Railan's fortress – an endless land of flickering lights, stretching out in all directions. The sensation of freedom had been overwhelming – never in my life had I been so far away from a wall.

Zaan chuckled. "It will take longer than tonight, at least," he said and pulled my hand.

ILYLLE'S EPILOGUE

I let him pull me out of his chamber and down the hall we'd fought in, all the way to my reception hall, with its throne and gilded doors.

Already, after only a few moments outside, my palace felt small. Or maybe *I* was bigger now – I looked over to Zaan, and was almost surprised to find myself still the same size, just a little taller than his shoulder. I smiled to myself at my foolishness, and then caught sight of his stern face as he turned to look at me. I straightened my shoulders and raised my chin.

"So what now?"

His lips curved, showing the tips of fangs. "In five hours you'll belong to Aranda – but until then, you to belong to me."

My magic pulsed through me in an almost physical wave. I looked around at the room. "Here?"

"Here," he said, voice low, and fell on me.

His arms wrapped me as his mouth met mine and I fell back under his weight – his tongue pushing mine, his hands at waist and breast – until my needs made me greedy and I was pushing him back, racing my hands up underneath pieces of his armor to feel skin and muscle underneath. Hands found buckles as fabric was torn, dropped, kicked, until we were naked in front of each other, our magic swirling around as our hands and mouths sought one another out. Fangs scraped my lips and I didn't care – I ran my hands up into his hair and held his mouth to mine, rubbing my whole body against him, elated to feel so much skin on skin. One of his arms held my back, the other hand cupped my ass, and between us his cock grew hard. I reached down to stroke it as he picked me up, stumbling the both of us toward a wall. I knew what he meant to do to me once we got there, so I pressed him back with my powers.

"Ilylle –" he protested – until he saw me kneel.

I took him in my mouth in the center of my throne room, and his hands clutched at my hair and shoulders as I sucked on him.

"Ilylle," he panted my name, looking down. He was so deliciously hard as I stroked my tongue along the bottom of his cock. He moaned low and his grip tightened, trying to pull me back on as I pushed off to talk.

"I could torment you for hours now, and it would still be fair."

He was almost swaying. "I've created a monster."

"You don't even know," I warned him, with a grin. He made a strangled sound, and then laughed, swooping down to pick me up.

This time I didn't fight him – I wanted to go wherever he led. He stormed us up to the dais where my throne was, set me down, and spun me, pushing me down over the seat with my ass still up. His hands kneaded me and I trembled, waiting for the moment when I would feel him push in – but it didn't come. Instead he knelt down, pushed my thighs wide, and started licking me my pussy from front to back.

I moaned and rose up on my tip-toes, bending further to show more of myself to him. He made animal sounds, lapping and sucking, as I cradled my breasts in their opposite hands, pulling at my own nipples to heighten each sensation. My body felt like it was spinning, as my voice rose in volume and my cries became more frequent, my legs shaking, my magic winding tight. Then he made a self-satisfied noise and pulled back, slapping my ass, hard.

Shocked back to reality I looked over my shoulder at him. "What was that?"

"A prelude to this," he said, standing, and he slid himself inside.

It was all I could manage to hold onto my throne as each of his thrusts rocked me. His cock found places in me I hadn't known before, his strokes stretching me wide – then he pulled back to tease me, bobbing his head in and out. I groaned and sank backwards, trying to taking more of him in, until he redoubled himself, holding onto the throne's back over my head. Each wave wound me tighter and all I wanted to do was scream – but then he reached down and grabbed hold of my hair, roughly hauling me up to hold me to his chest.

"Do you feel taken now, my Queen?" he rumbled in my ear.

It was all I could do to nod. My whole body was ready, waiting, starved.

"Good," he murmured, and pulled out.

It was my turn to make a strangled sound. "Not again, Zaan –" I said, stumbling forward without him.

"Definitely not," he said, moving to my side, pulling me in front of him as he sank to sit atop the throne. He rocked his hips forward as his cock jutted up and reached for my hips – I gathered his intent and straddled him and the throne awkwardly, thighs spread wide. I reached for the throne's back to lift myself up and he reached between us to guide himself back inside.

I moaned as I lowered down, feeling him settle himself back in where he belonged, where it was right. I squeezed my ass and thighs to pulse up and down, as he reached a hand between us to play a thumb on my bright spot. I gasped and started rolling against him, riding my hips into his, suddenly in charge, rocking up and down with infinitely small thrusts.

The way we were seated negated our difference in heights. I could see deep into his eyes, watch each sensation I gave him as it crossed his face, feel his breath on my lips. His free hand held my back, pressing me to him, and my hands were on his shoulders holding on.

He rocked me back then, and brought his mouth to my left breast, licking the margins of its curve, rolling my nipple against his tongue. I watched him, jaw dropped, breathing hard and pulsing, always pulsing – I didn't want anything to change ever, I wanted to be in this moment for the rest of my life. He nuzzled his face against me and turned his attention to my other breast, biting it a little harder, as if warning me. And then his hand pushed up into my hair and he brought me close, pulling my head gently to one side. I knew what was coming and knowing that made me ecstatically tense – I'd never felt so alive as I did that very moment, pushed to the brink of release and then dancing on its fine line.

"Ilylle," he whispered, and then sank his mouth against me, his lips finding my neck, me braced against his cock as his teeth went in.

I was still and made small noises then, feeling the sharpness of his teeth and the wet heat of his tongue. It hurt but it felt holy – I was sharing my essence with him. I kept gasping each time his mouth sucked and I knew my blood was thick inside his mouth – the same way his cock was thick inside of me. My hips started moving on their own. He growled without releasing me, biting harder as I desperately rubbed against his thumb.

I wound my hands in his hair, holding him tight and he made another growling sound. Both his hands found my hips and he braced his back against the throne and started fucking me, raising me up, pinned on him, thrusting fast. I cried out and held on, rubbing myself against him bodily, my breasts against his chest, his hands clawed around my ass, feeling every piece of his cock thrust inside, my magic winding around both of us like a hand –

"Zaan –" I cried out his name as my breath hitched and my magic pulled. Everything went silent and pure – there was no throne beneath us, no walls around, we were surrounded by a shimmering brilliant ball of light.

And then I cried out his name again and reality returned. "Zaan!"

I shuddered over him, my whole body wracked with electric sensations, as he kept thrusting wildly into me, until he released my neck to call my name.

"Ilylle," he groaned, pulling me near and pushing himself deep.

His cock stirred inside me and he thrust again – "Yes – Ilylle –" and then he gasped, rocking his head back, and gasped again. "Oh, Ilylle –" he panted, his chest heaving beneath my hands.

He held me to him, surrounding me with his arms, pulling me close. I could smell the sweat of his exertion – so unlike Joshan – and feel the wetness of his seed leaking out from between our bond. "Oh, my Queen," he whispered in my ear.

"My King," I whispered back, kissing his chin and neck.

ZAAN'S EPILOGUE

I pulled her out of the chamber where I'd been trapped as stone, away from her memories and Yzin. We needed to break new ground, start somewhere fresh that was only ours – so I pulled her past the hall we'd fought in and beyond her great chamber's door, down to the reception hall.

Every footstep made me throb – I had a low ache that needed answering. After nearly being pulled apart in Railan's dungeon I felt starved – and all of me needed to feed.

When we reached the center of the room I turned and caught her smiling at me. Little did she know the things I wanted to do to her.

"So what now?" she asked, acting bold.

I smiled wickedly. "In five hours you'll belong to Aranda – but until then, you to belong to me."

I felt her magic ripple through her, answering mine.

"Here?" she asked.

"Here," I said, prepared to take her.

My arms wrapped around her as my head leaned down. Her lips parted and let my tongue in – we were tasting one another in an instant, touching one another in an instant more, both of us wanting to finally know the other. I grabbed hold of the fabric of her dress and tore it as her hands fluttered over the buckles of my armor, undoing them haphazardly. Her hands found my skin as my hands found hers – the curve of her hips, the swell of her ass, always our mouths locked, tongues pressing. She put her hands in my hair and shivered against me as we freed ourselves from the final bits of cloth and I could feel her nipples pebble as they touched and feel the softness of her mound press in – my cock stiffened, and she reached between us to stroke it. I picked her up and started moving us toward a wall, but her magic fought mine to keep me still.

"Ilylle –" I warned – she couldn't possibly know how much I needed her right now, how badly I needed her blood to satisfy me and more – and then she knelt.

I groaned as her lips parted and she took me in. Without thinking I started to sway in time, rocking my hips against her as she sucked. My hands wound into her hair or clutched her shoulders, trying to hold on.

"Ilylle," I panted, looking down as she looked up, stroking her tongue against the bottom of my cock. I moaned again as she pulled back. I felt her rock, and tried in vain to keep her there.

"I could torment you for hours now, and it would still be fair."

My hips swayed involuntarily. "I've created a monster."

"You don't even know," she warned me with a grin. I didn't need games – I muttered a curse, then laughed, swooping down to pick her up.

This time she didn't fight me. I knew this time, she'd be mine.

I carried her up the dais to where the throne was and set her down, arranging her how I liked – pushing her back down and her ass up as she stood before the throne. I stood there for a moment, admiring everything about her, the spill of her hair, the curve of her hips. I could take her now – or I could choose to worship her some.

I took her ass in both my hands and felt her tremble and brace, assuming I would soon push in. Instead, I knelt behind her, pushed her thighs wide, and lapped at her with my tongue.

The sound she made then – it was exquisite, half a gasp, half a groan, as my tongue worked her over, my face pressed in. I sucked on her and kissed her pussy deeply, pushing my tongue up. She kept moaning and rose up on her toes, bending further to show more of herself to me, no shame, no inhibition. Her eagerness drove me wild, and I licked harder, pressing more. Her legs started to shake and her magic wrapped around us – I groaned and pulled back, satisfied with what I'd done, and slapped her ass, hard.

Ilylle jumped forward, then looked back. "What was that?"

"A prelude to this," I said, sliding myself inside of her.

Her pussy fit my cock like a glove. She was so wet and hot and each time I thrust she held me tight – I wanted to be inside her, to stay inside her, to feel her always wrapped around me.

Did she want the same for me? I pulled my cock back and teased her entrance with it, bobbing the thickest part of my head in and out. She groaned and tried to sink backwards to take more of me – *yes* – I leaned over her to grab the back of the throne and use it to help me fuck her. Each thrust she cried out – each thrust I needed her more. She was close, I was close, but there were parts of me hungry yet – I reached down and grabbed hold of her long blonde hair, hauling her up against my chest.

"Do you feel taken now, my Queen?" I asked her.

She nodded with a whimper.

"Good," I said, and then pulled out.

She sagged without me there. "Not again, Zaan –"

"Definitely not," I promised her. I moved her to one side and sat, then brought her back in front of me. My cock was still hard, jutting out – I scooted my hips forward, and pulled her to me.

She realized my intent and straddled the throne, thighs spread wide, and reached for the throne's back to lift herself up and slowly lower herself down, as I reached between us to guide myself back inside her. I hissed as I felt her envelope me again, and licked my thumb, putting it between us for her to rub on.

She started pulsing up and down my shaft; I wanted to grab her shoulders and pin her there, keep myself buried deep, but watching the ecstatic concentration on her face as her pleasure roiled – I pulled her to me, wrapping all of me in her, skin against skin, feeling her rock up and down with a series of small thrusts, rubbing herself against me.

She would come like this if I let her, and part of me wanted to watch that, to feel her magic wash over me as she utterly let go – but the rest of me was hungry still. I rocked her back, and lowered my mouth to her left breast.

I knew how to be careful with my fangs if I wanted to be – I used my lips and tongue against her, searching, licking, feeling her nipple perk for me, begging me to suck it more. I devoured her carefully, there was no part of her breast that I didn't taste, and then I turned my attention to her other one, trying to be as precise, but losing myself as my cock grew harder, all of me knowing what would come next. Did she know? She had to – I brushed my teeth against her in warning, as she kept pulsing – the way she felt wound around my cock – if she came, I would too, and this moment would be lost. I pulled her close again and pushed a hand into her hair, pulling her head gently to one side, bringing my mouth to her neck.

"Ilylle," I whispered in warning, and then bit into her irresistible flesh.

She stiffened as my teeth pierced and made small noises as I was lost in blood. I'd heard of this my entire life, how the blood of your beloved was like the sweetest wine, and had thought the men who shared such stories mad. But now – running my tongue over the wounds that I'd made, pressing and sucking every drop she would give me – I felt intoxicated. And then – she began to move.

Her blood, hot in my mouth, and my cock, hot inside her, I growled in satisfaction, at how everything felt right. Her hands wound up into my hair to hold me at her neck as her hips began tightening.

I pressed back into the throne, taking her with me, so that I could brace myself up off the ground, and started pounding all of me inside her, my hands clenched around her ass. This redoubling of sensation – the taste of blood – the way her body pressed to mine – the growing tightness in her pussy – her magic squeezing hard –

"Zaan –" she cried out my name first, losing herself. Her magic lashed out around us like a storm of light, with us calm in the center. She called my name again – and my body answered.

I released my bite and thrust up into her tightness, as her pussy grabbed my cock and pulled – "Yes – Ilylle –" I gasped and emptied myself inside her. Every pull she made drew more from me, until my body had no more to give – everything was hers. "Oh, Ilylle –" I panted, and pulled her back to me. "My Queen," I whispered, knowing it was true.

"My King," she whispered back and kissed my jaw.

EPILOGUE

We stayed in one another's arms until we caught our breath and he slipped out of me. Getting off the throne was awkward – he helped me balance, then I stood naked in front of him, smiling down.

"Don't get used to that – it's my throne."

Zaan chuckled, coming to a stand. "Don't worry – you're always welcome to sit on top of me," he said, and then kissed me hard. I sank back when he was through, feeling warm. He changed to smoke for an instant – as did his clothing – and then he was assembled again.

"That's unfair."

"You're the one who bathed already," he said waving his hand about to indicate my magic, and I laughed.

"Why here, Zaan? Why not my bed?" I asked, bending over to sweep up what was left of my dress. He watched all of me as I moved, eyes bright.

"I wanted you to claim this place as yours before emissaries arrive at dawn."

"There is no part of Aranda that is not mine," I said, with heavy irony, coming near. He held his hand out to me and I took it.

"Soon all of it will be honestly, for as long as you desire. But I thought making new memories here, to replace the old, would be a good choice."

I smiled up at him. "You make an excellent King."

He lifted my hand to his lips and kissed it.

I spun around, looking at all the screens. Soon I wouldn't need them anymore – I would be able see the entire outside world – I would meet my people, and my people would meet me. I would know if Mazaria still starved, and be in charge of fixing it if they did – and if all of Yzin's screens had told the truth, there was so much corruption and evil to uproot and replace with something better – it might take another twenty-thousand years to fix what Railan had done. And there was still the matter of all the Zaibann other trapped in stone – was there a way to release them, safely?

Zaan was right – this was my last night before I became Queen in earnest, when my country and my people would weigh on every waking thought. Which was finally as it should be, yes, but – I looked up to him and felt my magic stir anew. I straightened my back and took on a regal appearance for a second, before giving him a wicked grin.

"My King, how much time do we have left before morning?"

His eyebrows rose and he smirked, reveling the tip of one fang. "Enough, my Queen, enough," he said and pulled me in.

THANKS FOR READING Her Future Vampire Lover! This book is one of my favorites, I hope you enjoyed it too! Please keep reading through for the introduction of Blood of the Pack: Dark Ink Tattoo Book One.

I HEARD an engine turn the corner, startled, and the MMA fighter I was touching up a truly regrettable tribal tattoo on yelped.

"Sorry. Spine," I apologized, peeking over his hulking shoulder to see Jack Stone arrive on time for work, possibly for the first time ever while in my employ. His black 1963 Lincoln Continental swooped through Dark Ink's parking lot like a hearse.

Just Jack. I knew what his car sounded like. Even though our shifts didn't overlap often – I'd heard it often enough to know it wasn't a bike. And still....

I sprayed my client's shoulder with cool water and wiped the blood away, trying to ignore the slight jitter in my hand. This was my job – this was my tattoo-shop – and I'd been doing tats for the past seven years in peace. I breathed deep and willed myself calm. I wasn't scared and I hadn't lost control, and if I kept telling myself that long enough eventually I might believe it.

I put the heel of my hand on the fighter's back to steady it and stepped on the pedal to get the gun roaring again, starting where I'd left off, cleaning up some cheaper artist's shoddy job. In no other profession was the phrase 'you get what you pay for' so true.

This time, the fighter twitched, not me. No way not to hit nerves when you were tattooing someone over bone. Tattoos on top of bone felt like you were getting stabbed.

A lot like getting menacing letters from your ex in prison.

FIVE MINUTES LATER, Jack was leaning over from the wrong side of the counter, purring my name. "Angela."

I didn't turn around. I knew where he was, of course, I'd just made it a habit to ignore him. Mostly.

"Hey, boss-lady, I'm on time, just like you asked," he tried again. I snorted, stopped working, and looked up.

A gaggle of barely-old-enough-to-be-in-the-shop girls flocked behind him, flipping through flash displays, clearly whispering to themselves about him. He was stare-worthy. If you were into tall, lean but muscular men, black hair, brown eyes, and full sleeve tattoos, Jack was your kind of guy. When our shifts overlapped I had to remind myself he was off limits the same way that ex-smokers have to remind themselves to forget about cigarettes. I knew it was for my own good – I'd quit men that were bad for me a long time ago – but that didn't make it any less hard.

It was also why I tried to ignore him. It was good for him sometimes.

"On time for once," I corrected him.

"It's winter," he said, like that was an explanation.

I saw the post office truck pull into the parking lot behind him and my stomach clenched. "Yeah, of course," I said without thinking, standing and pulling my gloves off. "Wrap him up, will you?" I said, sidling towards the hip-high swinging saloon door that divided our half of the shop from the client's.

"My pleasure," Jack said, setting his ass down on the piercing display case and spinning his legs over to switch sides. Normally I'd yell at him about that, but – I reached the door just as the postman did, opening it up to take our letters from him.

Junk mail, tattoo convention flyers, the electricity bill and – something stamped 'Approved by the LVMPD'.

Goddammit.

I bit my lips and ran for the office. I stopped myself from slamming the door, just barely, instead whirling to place my back against it, like that would help keep all the monsters at bay, and slowly sank to the floor.

I threw the rest of the mail to the ground and opened up Gray's letter.

Visit me.

Funny how it only took two words to blow my life apart. I bit the side of my hand to stop from screaming – but somewhere on the inside, a hidden part of me howled.

I tore his letter up – same as I'd torn the other three I'd gotten, starting two weeks ago, and threw the pieces of it into the trash. If only escaping Gray were so easy. I should've left years ago – given myself and Rabbit a head start – but then what? Keep running forever? When I knew Gray and the Pack would always be able to find us? No, instead I'd pretended that I'd had a normal life – that I was normal. I'd rolled the dice, praying that someone meaner and nastier than Gray would take him out in prison.

I should've known that no such person existed.

I'd lived in Vegas my whole life – you'd think by now I'd be a better gambler.

There was a quiet knock on the door behind me. "Boss-lady?" Jack's voice, full of concern.

I stood and straightened myself out, opening the door a crack. "I, uh, didn't know what to charge him – so I asked for two-fifty. That enough?" Jack asked.

It was way more than I'd have asked for. It was only a touch up, hadn't even taken an hour. "He paid that?"

"I can be very convincing," he said, and shrugged, searching what he could see of me with his expressive eyes.

"Stop that. If I wanted to tell you about it, I would."

He leaned forward and pressed the door open. I could've fought back – could've closed the door – but I didn't want to make a scene. But my office was meant for only one person, one desk, one chair, there was no way for us be in here and not be in one another's space. In other circumstances I'd thought about doing things to Jack in here that'd make even the most jaded local blush, but now – I'd much rather he hold me and lie to me that everything was going to be all right.

"What was that?" he said, jerking his chin at the other mail still littering the floor.

"Nothing."

He stared me down. Could he really read me? Or was he just one of those guys who made you think they could? The kind you had relationships with where you filled all the silences with too much hope?

"Seriously, Ang," he said, his voice low.

I gestured to include the entire parlor. "It all says it's for me."

"Even the one from the Las Vegas Metropolitan police department?" he asked. "Don't ask me how I know what stamped mail from prison looks like."

Damn, Jack being Jack. Too smart for his own good. "It's none of your business," I said, as boss-like as I could, shutting down the conversation.

Jack took his cue. "All right, all right,"

"And I need to go."

"Yeah, to your date, I know."

I hadn't told him I was going on a date tonight, that that was why I needed him to really-I-mean-it be on time for once. And he'd said it with almost precisely flat inflection, so I couldn't really tell if he was jealous or whatever – and it didn't matter, because I was with Mark now, anyhow. But some deep and secret part of me bared its teeth and wagged its tail.

He glanced down at the letters. "If anything bad comes of that, you let me know, okay?"

"Sure," I lied, and pushed past him, out the door.

IF YOU'D LIKE to read more, hit up Blood of the Pack: Dark Ink Tattoo Book One

IF YOU WANT to read more hot books – and who doesn't? – the best way to keep track of my fiction is to join my mailing list: mailing list.

AS ALWAYS, if you're happy, tell a friend – or tell the whole internet, and leave a review. These matter more than you know (plus encourage me to write more quickly.)

IF YOU'D LIKE to read some of my other hot fiction, my most up-to-date bibliography is here and below!

WRITTEN with Kara Lockharte (and possibly as our co-author name, Cassie Lockharte):

The Prince of the Other Worlds Series – hot, sexy urban fantasy

Dragon Called

Dragon Destined

Dragon Fated

Dragon Mated

The Wardens of the Other Worlds Series – hot, sexy paranormal romance

Dragon's Captive

Wolf's Princess

Written as Cassie Alexander:

The Dark Ink Tattoo series – very, very hot paranormal romance

Blood of the Pack

Blood at Dusk

Blood at Midnight

Blood at Moonlight

Blood at Dawn

The House – a find your fantasy erotica

The House

Her Future Vampire Lover — futuristic vampire paranormal romance

Her Future Vampire Lover

Rough Ghost Lover — a sizzling paranormal erotica — DOES NOT HAVE HEA

Rough Ghost Lover

The Edie Spence urban fantasy series

Nightshifted

Moonshifted

Shapeshifted

Deadshifted

Bloodshifted

Printed in Great Britain
by Amazon

17156965R00103